"I've lost my son."

She gasped for air. Tried to think straight, tried to remain calm, but it was all impossible. "He's two. Please." She bit back hysteria. "Help me."

"Ma'am, I'm sure he's been found and taken outside. Go outside and wait."

"Wait?" It was the second time she'd heard it and this time she could take no more. "My son is missing!" She clenched her fists, driving her recently home-manicured nails into the palms of her hands. A sharp pain ran up her arms. It grounded her, temporarily dispelled the blinding panic.

Her hands shook and her head pounded. She wouldn't give up. Coming to Marrakech had been a decision made in desperation. For it was here, in the land of the sheiks, where she searched for the lifeline that would protect her heart. Only one man could save her son and keep them both safe.

She needed to find Sheik Talib Al-Nassar. But first she had to find Everett. He was her heart, and without him, there was nothing.

SON OF THE SHEIK

RYSHIA KENNIE

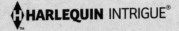

HARLEQUIN INTRIGUE®

When I was a toddler, you read endlessly to me and then wondered why I became a bookworm. I suppose that makes you partially responsible for the writer I am. You taught me how to read and you also taught me self-reliance. If it can be bought, it can be made. From soup to wedding veils. For my mother, who reminds me every day that nothing is impossible. *Quit* just isn't in her vocabulary. To you, Mom.

ISBN-13: 978-1-335-72106-8

Son of the Sheik

Copyright © 2017 by Patricia Detta

Recycling programs for this product may not exist in your area.

Printed in U.S.A.

HARLEQUIN®
www.Harlequin.com

Ryshia Kennie has received a writing award from the City of Regina, Saskatchewan, and was also a semifinalist for the Kindle Book Awards. She finds that there's never a lack of places to set an edge-of-the-seat suspense, as prairie winters find her dreaming of warmer places for heart-stopping stories. They are places where deadly villains threaten intrepid heroes and heroines who battle for their right to live or even to love. For more, visit ryshiakennie.com.

Books by Ryshia Kennie

Harlequin Intrigue

Desert Justice

Sheik's Rule
Sheik's Rescue
Son of the Sheik

Suspect Witness

CAST OF CHARACTERS

Sheik Talib Al-Nassar—An investigator with Nassar Security, he works and plays hard. When he arrives at his friend's hotel he finds not only the aftermath of an explosion in the lobby but also one of his ex-girlfriends, with a baby in tow. Faced with a situation that could turn tragic, he has no time to consider her unexpected arrival or her surprising situation. But it's soon clear that Sara needs him, and he'll do everything in his power to keep her safe.

Sara Elliott—Left the ashes of her life in the United States and ran with her toddler to foreign soil. But an explosion in the hotel she's staying at has her turning to the only man who might keep them safe. Talib is her last resort and the only man who endangers everything she holds dear.

Everett Elliott—The toddler's engaging antics could steal your heart, but it's his life that may be on the line.

Sheik Faisal Al-Nassar—He runs the Wyoming branch of Nassar Security. The information he provides is troubling.

Ian Hendrik—He went against Talib's advice when he opened his hotel before all security measures were in place. What does he know of the explosion that followed?

Tad Rossi—He dated Sara once. Now there's something else he wants from her.

Sheik Emir Al-Nassar—Talib's older brother cannot believe that Talib doesn't see the truth.

Habib Kattanni—He went to school with Talib, but he shares more with him than just an upper-crust education.

Prologue

He slipped out of the back entrance of the Desert Sands Hotel and disappeared into the darkness. And, although he didn't move far away, he looked back only once, and with a self-satisfied smile. He had been in the hotel for a little over twenty minutes. It had all been too easy. He had come in through the unlocked fire exit where security cameras hadn't been installed. He didn't glance at the man at the front desk, for he knew that he had also been paid both for his assistance and his silence.

Neither of them would be here for the outcome. They only knew their parts, nothing more. He waited for the one other player in this game. She arrived exactly thirty minutes later, on schedule, as was her habit. Despite her initial reluctance, a doubling of the original sum was all that was required.

He glanced at his watch. It was five o'clock. He had ten hours before the second act.

He vanished into the narrow and twisted corridors of the Medina, where he had lived the majority of his life and where the plan had incubated. It was here where he would wait for his finale and then others would take charge. He was only a pawn in a much bigger game.

The signs of a new day merged into late morning and then followed into early afternoon. It wasn't until the day drifted close to midafternoon that the man from the Medina returned. And then he waited. There was no need to enter the hotel. Everything he needed would be brought to him, as planned.

THE FIRST SIGN of trouble went unnoticed by anyone in the lobby of the Desert Sands Hotel. The day began like any other, full of promise for business and tourists alike. The hotel was abuzz with the imminent arrival of a busload of tourists that would soon mesh with the energy of the guests already there. Times were changing and new ideas were being implemented. The hotel was under new ownership and so far, the change had been flawless. Everything was going as beautifully as the clear September day that held such promise for those eager to explore the city. Marrakech was full of places to discover, secrets waiting to be found. The city had an exotic history that was steeped in the depths of the Medina. There, the hustle and bustle in the souks, the numerous and varied shops with the merchants peddling their wares, added excitement and mystery, as had been the tradition for centuries. It was the place tourists came to spend good money and be part of that rich history. It was a special place, an exciting place. For most, it was very different from what they were familiar with. For others, it was a place of business—a place where commerce was at the center. For there was money here as well as history. There were other things, too, like poverty and crime, that lurked in the narrow alleys where he waited.

Now, near the heart of all that, the low ticking of an explosive device went unheard. It had been placed close to where the luggage rack was customarily parked. It hid in the far corner of the lobby, buried beneath the chatter of the guests and the stream of voices that kept the hotel running without a hiccup. The deadly, monotonous beat was too quiet to be heard or seen…yet.

Chapter One

Marrakech, Morocco
Tuesday 3:15 p.m.

At the Desert Sands Hotel registration desk, Sara Elliott laid her passport on the counter. She then set her two-year-old son beside it so that she could keep an eye on him while completing the hotel registration. It had been a long flight and they were both exhausted. Despite the fact that it was midafternoon, she was looking forward to getting a snack and then getting her son bathed, and both of them having a nap. Traveling over an ocean and between continents with a two-year-old was no picnic. Only her son had managed to sleep on the long flight from Maine to Marrakech. For her, there had been no pleasure in it, but rather, only an endurance test in a flight borne out of desperation.

She had her arm around her son's waist, for a hand on his leg wasn't enough. Everett was a busy little boy. He didn't like to sit still for any length of time and now was no different, as within seconds he was reaching for the registration pen. Then he poked the edge of the registration clerk's computer while endearing himself to the older couple beside her who were checking in, as well.

After a minute of that, his bottom lip began to quiver as he lost interest. She guessed that he was realizing that despite devouring two cookies on the ride between the hotel and the airport, he was hungry. She dug in her purse for his soother. He was too old for such a thing. That was what the latest parenting book she had read indicated, but they hadn't mentioned another option for situations such as these. The soother was immediately grabbed up in her son's chubby hand and popped into his mouth. Her nerves settled slightly. Now she had a few minutes of peace. Time to get them registered and settled in their room.

She closed her purse, using one hand to steady her son as she juggled the diaper bag that was over one shoulder, along with her carry-on bag and purse. She fisted the hotel pen in an attempt not to drop it when what sounded like outrageously loud fireworks went off behind her.

She jumped and dropped her purse onto the counter. The hand holding her son remained, instinctively, protectively, there. Someone screamed and a man shouted. The registration clerk jumped back, shock in his dark eyes. Smoke immediately began to fill the room and it was unclear what had happened.

She pulled her son off the counter, holding him tight against her side, his legs dangling. She turned to see what was going on, and one of the three bags she carried caught on the thin wooden panel that acted as a counter divider. Her carry-on twisted and wrapped around her arm, locking her in position. Smoke was billowing from the corner of the lobby, where the suitcase trolley was, and a small fire was licking at a couple of the bags. The smoke only added to the confusion because minutes earlier, the lobby had been flooded with an influx of tourists that had just gotten off a tour bus.

There was chaos in the haze, as people began to run for the exit. They pushed through the crowded area where others stood, stunned. She could see that the window that faced the parking lot had been blown out. A bomb, she thought with shock, and then realized that it was an outrageous idea.

It was seconds before the reality of what had just happened seemed to hit her full-force. They needed to get out of here. Who knew what might follow. There could be another explosion, a larger fire. The situation was unpredictable and dangerous. She'd wasted precious seconds. Her son was in her arms, but her important documents were in the bag caught on the counter. She wasn't frightened enough to leave the bag behind, at least not yet. For without their passports and travel documents…she couldn't think of it. But she also couldn't hold her son any longer and continue to juggle her bags. She put Everett back down on the counter. His hands immediately went over his ears as he sniffled, but didn't start crying.

A woman jostled Sara and when the fire alarm began to bleat it was somehow unexpected and she let out a small involuntary scream. Everett immediately followed her example, as he always did, his soother now clutched in his chubby fist.

Darn it, she thought. But she couldn't have bit back her reaction, it was as involuntary as every other shriek that had run through the room.

"It's all right," Sara said quickly, not knowing how all right it might be. She held him in place with one hand while with the other she tried to free the caught bag. Her purse banged against her hip as Everett began to wail.

A short, thick woman pushed past her, herding a trio of children, knocked her elbow and threw her completely off balance. She staggered against the counter and noticed, while not really acknowledging, that all the staff had now vacated their posts.

A snowy-haired man with a pleasant expression and eyes that crinkled with concern approached her. "Here, let me help you." He reached for Everett. "Let's get you out of here," he said to her son.

Everett stopped crying long enough to look at the man and held his tiny arms out.

"No!" The word was sharper, louder and fiercer than she intended.

She guessed that he didn't mean any harm. Still, despite everything, she wasn't taking any chances. The thoughts ran rapidly through her mind and she considered the possibility that he might really just want to help. The offer seemed suspect, but he was from a generation where helping someone with their child was natural. The simple kindness did not place you immediately in a lineup as a suspect to potential kidnapping, as it did today.

He looked at her and moved to her other side. "I'm sorry. You just looked like you had your hands full." He reached over and unhooked her bag. "That should help."

She looked at him sheepishly. "Thank you," she said as the man nodded and moved on. And she was thankful in more ways than one, for despite the noise and confusion, Everett had stopped crying.

She lifted her son, who, at thirty-two pounds, was a good size for a two-year-old. Normally she had a stroller, but that was somewhere with the luggage, what might be left of it. She had no choice but to carry him.

"It'll be all right," she whispered to him and wasn't sure if that helped. She was just glad he hadn't let out a howl of outrage. Instead, his arms were around her in a death grip and he was sucking his soother again. If her arms stopped shaking she'd be all right. But the man was right about one thing—they needed to get out of here. The smoke was swirling through the lobby, making it almost impossible to see to the other side, where their luggage was, or to her left, where the exit was.

She moved forward. She meant to follow the crowd to the exit, when the stairwell door opened and people streamed out as they began to come down from the upper floors. The hotel lobby was suddenly not just busy but congested to the point that no one could move. Everett twisted in her arms, trying to get down, and with her arms still shaking, his squirming made him difficult to hold. The soother was gone. It must have dropped. She looked down but there was nothing but smoke and chaos. He began to cry, she imagined more from frustration than fright.

"No, sweetie. You can walk once we're outside." She tightened her grip as his cries threatened to match the noise of the fire alarm.

"Ma'am," the concierge said, taking her by the elbow. "You've got to leave now. Get the little one out of here."

"Yes," she agreed as she fumbled, the pull on her elbow the final straw to her already shaky grip that was weakening the more Everett squirmed.

"Mama!" he yelled.

"We're going, Ev. We're going." But she wasn't so sure as Everett twisted again and slid halfway down her chest.

The concierge had already moved on, unaware that his actions had loosened her hold on her son. She struggled to get a better grip on him, but he was slipping further. It was all made worse by the crowd as they jostled them this way and that. Someone knocked her left side and this time she lost her grip. She didn't have any choice but to either drop Everett, or set him down.

She placed him on the ground, her hand on his shoulder as she stood up. But the split second between that and when she reached down to take his hand found her fishing for air. She looked down. In the space of a second he had disappeared. There was nothing but a sea of people amidst the chaos of noise and smoke. Her heart raced.

A woman screamed.

To her right, in a thick cloud of smoke, something tipped and crashed to the floor. There was another scream. This time she realized that it was her. Panic threatened to engulf her. She couldn't let it. She had to find Everett.

Through a break in the smoke, she could see that the flames were licking one corner of the wall behind where the suitcase trolley had been standing. Shock raced through her at the fire and at the thought that everything she had brought was more than likely about to be, or already was, destroyed. But the thought was fleeting, for none of that mattered. She had to find Everett.

A man with a hotel employee jacket rushed forward with a fire extinguisher. He blasted the flames that were eating up the wall. Another employee attacked the flames that were threatening one suitcase with a dripping wet towel. But his attempts only caused the fire to move from one area to another. Clothes were strewn around the luggage rack. It was obviously an explosive device of some type, at least that's what her suspicious and slightly hyperactive mind thought. It was a strange thought, considering the panic that was filling her every second that went by. Instead, she saw trivial details like that. Details that meant nothing when the entire hotel could go up in flames at any moment and her son was nowhere in sight.

"Everett!" she screamed.

To her right she distinctly heard a woman's unpleasant voice tell her to shut up. She swung around. She was facing the opposite way that the crowd was moving. She'd been oblivious to the danger to herself, or the obstruction she was to others. It was like she faced the enemy alone, as the crowd seemed to act like one beast racing for the main exit.

She looked down, as if expecting to see Everett right there, right at her side where he should be. Instead, she bumped elbows with a matronly woman, who pushed past her, causing her to stumble. A man shoved by on her other side and as he did, he tripped and caught himself as he grabbed her arm, before he righted himself and disappeared into the smoke.

"Have you seen a little..."

She was shoved from the side as more people emerged from the stairwell and headed for the exit. Water began to spray from the overhead sprinklers.

"Ma'am," a man said. Her burning eyes could barely make out the uniform, but it was a hotel employee, and all she could think was that finally there was help.

"My son..." she began. "I've lost my baby!" The words came out in a panicked shriek. She'd lost control. She was beyond words. She had to get it together. She had to find him.

"You're going to have to leave," he said as he pushed her forward toward the exit.

"No!"

His grip on her elbow tightened. Now he was pulling her toward the exit.

"No!" This time it was more forceful and she considered that she might have to do something violent if he didn't let go, like kick him in the shins. Something. "I've lost…"

"Ma'am." He kept walking, dragging her along. "This is an urgent situation. You need to leave now. The emergency crews will handle it. You're making it difficult for the others, blocking the exit."

"What? My—"

"Out!" he said shortly, obviously losing patience with her.

She was ready to smack him if that was what it took. Instead they were pushed from behind and his grip loosened. She pulled free of him, backed up and dodged her way through the stampede.

"Everett!" she shrieked.

"Get moving!" someone else snarled as they shoved past her.

She gagged on smoke. She imagined her baby struggling to breathe. She imagined him trampled as people pushed their way out of the hotel.

She tried to call his name again but her throat was dry and tight. She coughed. He could be crushed. He was so small, too small. How had she lost him? She was a horrible mother and, despite everything that had happened, she was more frightened than she'd ever been in her life.

Someone rammed her shoulder. She was knocked off balance. She staggered, fighting to prevent herself from falling. Yet even as her hand hit the carpet, she was still frantically scanning the area. In fact here, low to the ground, she could see better, for the smoke was less dense and she was at his height, the height of a two-year-old. She was also in danger of being trampled, as she was sure he was. She swallowed against the panic and smoke that was locking her throat. Her voice was all she had—he had to hear her. For there was danger everywhere and he was alone.

Sirens were wailing in the distance, the haunting call both frightening and hopeful. Would they get here in time? They had to. She had to find him. She would find him. There was no other outcome, not one that she could survive.

"Everett," she croaked as she stood up and elbowed her way against the crowd.

Where could he be? Had someone taken him? It was another thought to cloud her mind with fear. It was a thought that taunted the mind of every parent. A fear fed by the media and that one never outgrew— the boogeyman in the closet.

But this time the boogeyman had gotten out! He had her son and her heart constricted at the thought. She bumped into a woman and pushed away from her without a second look. That wasn't her. She wasn't a rude, self-serving woman who shoved people to the side without an apology. It didn't matter. She was now. She'd be anything she needed to be if only she could find her little boy. She was bent low to the ground, not crawling, still standing and buffeted on either side by the relentless crush of panic rushing to escape.

"Crazy," someone muttered.

"Get out of my way," someone else said as a knee caught her shoulder and threatened to knock her off balance.

She stood up, saw another hotel employee and tried to make her way to him. "Help me," she said.

"Ma'am. You've got to leave."

"My son…"

She was thrown off balance as a tall, heavyset man, leading with his belly, knocked her aside as he headed for the exit.

It was impossible. She couldn't give up. She had to find him. Tears began to blur her vision and her head pounded from the smoke. What must he be feeling? She squinted in the murky lobby that oddly seemed clearer than it had only a minute ago.

She would die if she lost him. Her throat closed and smoke threatened to choke her, but she forged ahead.

Yet no matter how hard she fought against the tide of panicked hotel guests, her son was nowhere in sight. Her baby had disappeared!

"Everett!" Her son's name came out in a choked mockery of a shout. This wasn't happening! She hadn't come all the way to Morocco to lose him now, or for that matter, to lose him ever. She was here to make him safe, keep him safe. She'd given up a job, security, and now he was gone. This wasn't supposed to happen. This trip, the uncomfortable flight, all of it was supposed to result in her keeping him away from the danger that threatened him in the States. And now he was missing!

It was unbelievable. She took a deep breath and screamed his name. Smoke billowed around her and a man looked at her curiously.

"Can I help?"

"I've lost my son." She gasped for air. Tried to think straight, tried to remain calm, but it was impossible. "He's two. Please." She bit back tears. "Help me."

"Ma'am, I'm sure he's been found and taken outside. Go outside and wait."

"Wait?" It was the second time she'd heard it and this time she could take no more. Her voice was not the voice she told Everett to use on a regular basis, it was not her indoor voice. "My son is missing!" Her fists clenched, driving her recently home-manicured nails into the palms of her hands. A sharp pain ran up her arms. The pain grounded her, temporarily dispelled the blinding panic.

Her hands shook and her head pounded. She wouldn't give up. Coming to Marrakech had been a decision made in desperation. For it was here in the land of the sheiks, where she searched for the lifeline that would protect her heart. One man, who she held responsible for almost destroying her life, was now the only man who could save her son.

But now it didn't matter if she found Sheik Talib Al-Nassar. Only one thing mattered—finding Everett. He was her heart and without her son, there was nothing.

Chapter Two

Even for a car fanatic, one who had experienced the ultimate of vehicles, the BMW Z4 was a dream to drive. The car's custom paint job hinted at shades of an early morning sky. Its pearl-blue base and finishing coats were multi-layered and hand applied. The result gleamed in the sunlight. The butter-soft, smoke-gray leather steering wheel was almost erotic beneath his palm. While he'd owned and driven many luxury sports cars, this one was sweeter than any vehicle he'd had before. Just a slight touch of his hand on the wheel had the car responding. Even within the confines of the city, the vehicle was amazing. The engine purred like a satiated mountain cat. He could hardly wait to get it onto the open road and test its limits.

Talib Al-Nassar had the seat back as far as it would go, his left leg was stretched out and the warm fall air whispered across his cheek like a lover's caress. Poor analogy, he thought, reminded of his last lover. The BMW definitely scored higher points than she had. Ironically, she'd been rather like the rest, holding his attention for not much longer than it had taken to bed her. He supposed he deserved the playboy label his older brothers had given him. But the truth was that the women in his life wanted no more from the relationship than he was able to give them. It was only his brother Faisal who seemed to truly get it, but then Faisal, like him, was living what they called "the life." There was no woman to hold him to account, no children, and he wouldn't have it any other way. At twenty-nine, he just couldn't imagine being responsible for another human. It was unthinkable. And a woman... The thought dropped as he took a corner with ease and couldn't wait to get the speed up and test what this baby was capable of. He couldn't imagine a woman, no matter how beautiful or how arousing, ever matching the thrill that this BMW would give him. Only an hour ago he'd picked up the new car. He'd been looking forward to this for days. In fact, he had a road trip planned into the Atlas Mountains. He would visit an old friend and test the car's slick handling on the tight curves and bends of the mountain roads. But today he needed to stop by the hotel his friend Ian had just purchased. Ian had called wanting advice on getting the security in his hotel beefed up after a recent breach. It was only a favor between friends. It wasn't the usual kind of situation he dealt with as one of the executives of Nassar Security. The business was headed by his brother Emir and co-run by he and his brothers. It provided security and protection through branches in both Jackson, Wyoming, and here in Marrakech.

He doubted that this consultation would take any time at all as he was already familiar with the hotel's security. In fact, he anticipated that he might be able to convince Ian to go for a short test drive prior to tomorrow's excursion.

As the vehicle easily took the corner, its engine purring, he frowned.

"Bugger." He'd picked up the phrase on a recent trip to Australia and it had since become part of his vocabulary. His hands tightened on the wheel, the thrill of the car and the promise of speed and luxury it promised forgotten. Instead he was shocked first by the smell of smoke and then, as he turned another corner, by clouds of smoke filling the air.

"What's going on?" he muttered. For it looked like the hotel might be on fire, yet he couldn't see flames. What was clear was that smoke was billowing out of the door as fast as people were emerging. The fire alarm was shrilling down the street, cutting through the sounds of shouts and screams. In the distance, the sirens of the approaching emergency vehicles could be heard. He frowned as he gripped the wheel and assessed what he could of the situation from where he was. His phone was in his pocket but he hadn't received a call from Ian. That was understandable; whatever was going on, Ian would have his hands full.

Talib turned the vehicle smoothly into a parking space at the end of the block, leaving room for the emergency vehicles. He grabbed a bag from behind the seat that contained a few items that he'd often found indispensable. He pulled out one item that he hadn't thought he would need on a day where the upper-most thing on his mind was the joy of a new vehicle. The explosive detection device was more than likely over-kill, but one never knew.

Talib leaped out. A few men in hotel uniforms were directing the crowd, keeping them on the side-walk, out of the way of the imminent approach of emergency crews. Up ahead he saw one hotel em-ployee moving among the crowd, laying a hand here, offering a word there. Another was passing out water bottles. He looked over and saw an older woman lean-ing against a vehicle as another staff member held her shoulder, obviously trying to calm her. Ian's staff were well trained. His friend had followed the advice that Talib had given all those months ago, when Ian had first mentioned that he was planning to get into the hotel business.

Things were chaotic but seemed under control. No one seemed to be in imminent danger—at least here, outside the hotel. It had taken him seconds to make that assessment as he strode the short distance to the hotel entrance. Now within yards of the front door, he was faced with a milling crowd that was not quite as organized or controlled as those he had just passed. He guessed that they'd just emerged from the build-ing and were still shocked, unsure of what they'd es-caped from, or what they had yet to face.

"Get away from the entrance!" he commanded, pointing to a green space just across the street. Half a dozen people followed his instruction, the rest con-tinued to mill where they were.

He directed more stragglers across the street. In one case, he took a woman's elbow and escorted her to the curb, where she finally managed to cross the street under her own steam. He'd had a lot of experience with this as he and his brothers had built Nassar Security into the powerhouse company that it was. He'd learned over the years that people often responded like herded animals in an emergency. They lost their individual ability to think.

His phone beeped.

"Yeah," he answered, knowing it was Ian. They spoke for less than a minute. In that time, Ian told him what he knew, that they believed there'd been an explosion and that it might be linked to a suspicious-looking man seen in the early morning hours by the hotel parking lot. That information had been revealed on the security footage Ian had just remotely accessed.

"When this is over..."

"We'll get you beefed up," Talib assured him. "I'm going in now."

His friend had confirmed that the explosion had been confined to one area of the lobby. Ian had been at an outside meeting, but was now en route. From what Ian had said, he estimated that his own arrival was five minutes after the explosion and now, from the sounds of the rapidly approaching sirens, minutes before emergency crews.

Talib considered the information he'd just received. Combined with what he knew of the security and the time line, he believed that there was only one perp responsible for planting the device. It wasn't easy to plant an explosive device undetected in a public area of a hotel. The time that had passed since the explosion backed up his preliminary theory that there was only one explosive device.

Explosives were used for any number of reasons. This one appeared to be small but he would see for himself in a minute. If that was the case, there was a good chance that this bomb had been set to make a statement, or had been used to create a distraction. Since the damage had been contained and been in an area that saw low traffic, he was led to believe that whoever had done this wasn't going for a high kill rate. It could be a grudge against the owner. The explosion hadn't been far-reaching enough to provide much of a killing field. Unless there was another explosive, or this one had been a screwup...

He strode through the hotel doors, which someone had had the foresight to prop open. Inside, the emergency procedures weren't quite so efficient, as he had to weave through a lobby still crowded with stragglers.

Traces of smoke swirled through the lobby, but he was immediately able to see where the explosion had been. Embers still burned in two ruined suitcases. Clothing was scattered everywhere. The metal suitcase trolley lay where it had tipped over. To his left, a woman, wearing only a bathrobe and flip-flops, tripped and stumbled. He was there in a flash. His reflexes were quick. They'd been honed by physical fitness and a regular baseball scrimmage with friends that occurred at least twice monthly. He had her elbow, and powered her toward the door, where he released her ten feet from the exit.

"Thank you." Her lips trembled but there was a stoic gleam in her eye. "I'm all right now."

He nodded but watched as she hurried past a hotel employee who was directing the remaining guests. He remained standing there, watching until she was safely out of the building.

He turned and scanned the lobby and saw a woman moving away from the crush and out of sight. She was wearing a maid's uniform. The dull beige material was designed to fade into the background, to provide service while flitting on the periphery. It was the perfect ensemble for what was intended, but now it seemed that blending in was giving her an advantage. The thought was one he tagged and filed away for later consideration; there were other things to concern himself with now. He was more interested in the explosion site and how someone had slipped in and out and planted the explosive unnoticed, than in the maid's uniform. He knew, from looking at the hotel plans, that a corridor led from the back of the lobby to conference rooms and a back exit. He was surprised that no one else seemed to be using that exit.

He activated the portable explosive detection device. As he moved slowly along the perimeter of the lobby with the device, he was cognizant of the rapidly thinning crowd. He was also aware that no one was acting suspiciously, but rather that there was still a great deal of confusion. People were almost spin-ning in circles as smoke continued to obscure the exit and the remaining staff seemed to have evacuated. So much for security measures, he thought, realizing that not everything he'd advised had been implemented. His attention returned to the device. The lobby wasn't officially clear of explosives yet, but he was reasonably sure that there wasn't another planted.

He moved away from the luggage and farther into the lobby. As he did, he looked down and saw a child's soother on the floor. That was odd. There weren't any children in sight. He didn't expect there to be. Even in chaos it seemed people managed to instinctively grab their children. He wasn't sure why, but he picked up the soother and put it in his pocket.

He looked up, thinking of the woman in the maid's uniform. She was the only one he'd seen using the back exit. His instincts, everything in his being, told him that something was off, that there was something more to this lone woman. Had she placed the explosive and come back to see the results of her work? Even as he considered that option he discounted it. Her mannerisms hadn't reflected anything nefarious.

As he made the decision to follow her, a woman's panic-torn voice sliced through both the chaos and his thoughts. It brought his attention, to the lobby.

"Everett!"

The voice sounded familiar, even muted by the chaos of sounds that swirled around him. He didn't have time to analyze it. Instead, he moved deeper into the lobby, turning left and following the path of the maid he'd seen head in that direction. He turned a corner in the corridor and that's when he saw her. She was holding a small boy by the wrist, causing him to stand on tiptoes. The child's cheeks were wet from crying and he had his free thumb in his mouth. She was wearing a cream-colored head scarf and the beige uniform he'd caught a glimpse of earlier. Nothing about her seemed out of the ordinary. It appeared only that she was leading a child to safety.

But his gut told him that something was very wrong. "What are you doing with him?" he asked in Arabic. He doubted that the child was hers. No worker would have brought their child to work.

His theory was justified by the look of panic in her eyes and the way she held the boy by the wrist rather than by his hand. Clearly, she was unfamiliar with children that young, the panic obvious in her entire demeanor. He supposed his size and the fact that he was carrying an unconcealed firearm made him look official. Police, she might be thinking, although it wasn't true.

"Where did you get him?" he asked without explaining who he was. He acted on his first hunch. "He's not yours." Aggression could work to his advantage in this instance.

Her mouth tightened and her eyes darted, as if she was seeking an escape.

He strode forward and kneeled down in front of the child, who now had half of his free fist stuck in his mouth. His face was smeared with what looked like dirt and streaked with tears. His dark hair curled wildly in every direction, but his shimmering light brown eyes looked at Talib with more curiosity than fright.

Talib stood up. He wasn't sure what was happening here, but he intended to get to the bottom of it.

"A man said his wife had taken him. He paid me to deliver him to the back exit." She clasped her hands and backed up. "I…" She stumbled, speaking in Arabic. "It was easy to take him. There was so much running, screaming."

"You took him in the confusion?" he asked.

She nodded. "I don't understand much English and that's what he—" she pointed at the child "—speaks. Although he can't speak much, he keeps saying Mama." She looked genuinely frightened and possibly even sorry. "I…something was wrong. I was going back to the desk to tell Mohammed," she said.

"Who's Mohammed?" Talib asked and made no effort to filter the edge from his voice.

"My supervisor," she said anxiously.

"How much money were you offered?"

"None. I wouldn't—"

"If you want to keep your job…" He let the threat dangle. He was beginning to lose patience with the whole situation. "Look, I assume you need the money but this kid isn't the way you're going to get it."

"He said he was his father. I needed the money. But I was going to take him back." She shook her head and looked down at the boy.

"You were doing the right thing," Talib said, strangely believing her. Poverty could cause good people to do desperate things. And in Morocco, the father's rights could still often trump those of the mother. It was possible that she truly thought she was bringing the boy to his father. Possible, but unlikely. He squatted down and picked up the child.

"I'll take it from here," he said with the voice of authority that was never questioned. "I'm sure his mother is beside herself with worry." The woman's story had rung true and odds were that she was struggling to feed a family, possibly extended family, on a maid's wages. Still, she had taken this child, and in ordinary circumstances he would have detained her. He shifted the toddler on one arm just as the panic in her eyes flared and she bolted. He had no choice but to let her go.

He looked down at the child in his arms and was met by curious eyes that looked at him in an oddly familiar way. "You've had quite the day, little man," he said. The toddler smiled and pushed a finger against his chin.

But as he reentered the lobby, a scream rose above the alarms and the sirens of the emergency vehicles that had just arrived.

A woman charged through the throng of people, heading straight toward him.

"Everett!" she screamed.

She was a petite whirlwind. She was moving so fast, so ferociously, that there was little doubt that she was emotionally invested, that the child was hers. There was also no doubt that he knew her.

He allowed the child to be plucked from his arms. She held the boy so tightly that he began to cry, but it was the panicked look in her gray eyes and a vision from long ago that registered with Talib. He shoved the disconcerting memory away. What mattered most was getting the two of them out of here. Smoke still filled the area. Firefighters were just entering the lobby and were already directing the remaining guests outside.

"Let's go," he ordered. It didn't matter why she was here or even who she'd been to him. He needed to get her and the boy he assumed was her son to safety.

"What were you doing with him?" she demanded. Her eyes pinned his like a thick gray mist and were the first warning that she was dangerously angry.

It was similar to the last time he'd seen those eyes.

Except, the last time she had only recently left the bed that was still warm from their lovemaking. He remembered that she'd given him a dreamy look and told him that she loved him. He didn't like to think about that moment, for he wasn't proud of how he'd reacted.

It hadn't gone well after that, after what he had said.

She'd been proud and angry and told him what she'd thought of him, which hadn't been at all flattering. He'd said nothing, for there'd been nothing to say. Every word she'd spoken had been the truth. After that, he'd driven her home in a car that was thick with silence. He was sorry, but at the time what he had told her had been the truth. It was what he'd told every woman who'd fancied him. He wasn't ready to settle down, be serious, or declare undying love for anyone.

He doubted that he ever would. Unfortunately, he'd told her that. It was then that she had tried to kill him with a look deadlier than he'd ever seen. Then, she'd managed to chip the custom paint job on that year's vehicle when she'd kicked the door with one tiny, stiletto-clad foot. To her credit, he didn't think it was deliberate. But he had his doubts. Especially because she'd done all that while telling him in a deadly calm voice that he could go to a place where it was just a bit hotter than the Sahara in midsummer.

It hadn't been his best breakup.

Chapter Three

"Sara?"

The voice was filled with that deep, command-ing ring that she had never forgotten. It peeled back the layers of panic, penetrated the emotional chaos of losing Everett and her maternal fussing that she couldn't stop. For the first time that tone, that sense of self and of control, didn't grate, but instead was a life raft in a sea of insanity. The tone cut through everything and his presence broke easily through the crowd. She knew his voice like she knew her own heartbeat, would always know it, could never forget it.

He was back and he'd brought her son, when she had thought that her baby was lost. There was only one thing important in this moment—getting Everett out of the hotel.

"Are you all right, baby?"

She ran her hands over her child as if she expected to find a fatal wound, a broken bone or some injury equally as threatening. There was nothing. Only a nose that was running and eyes that were red and, oddly, a smile on his face.

She fumbled in her pocket for a tissue, pulled it out and wiped her son's nose, not slowing her stride as she headed for the door. Everett pulled away to look over her shoulder and what he saw made him giggle. At least her son was finding some amusement in a situation that was causing her empty stomach to want to heave. She clutched him tighter and walked faster.

Talib.

She could feel him right behind her and to her left. He wasn't saying anything, but his presence was insuring that there was no delay in exiting the building.

She hadn't seen him since that fateful summer almost three years ago. She'd hoped never to see him again and yet here she was looking for his help.

Despite coming here to find him, she hadn't been prepared for it to happen like this. Just his presence brought back all the hurt. She'd been afraid of that. That was one of the reasons she hadn't wanted to come here in the first place. There'd been many reasons, but that one had trumped them all. But she'd had no choice. She was here, with him right behind her. The hurt flooded back strong enough to steal her breath, like a tsunami from which she could never escape and with it came the anger.

Her heart pounded. For even after the years that had stretched between them, he affected her. He'd been a first-class jerk and one wasn't apt to forget such a man. But now there was one other thing that she wasn't apt to forget. He'd saved the most important thing in her life. Saved, found—she wasn't sure which was accurate and it didn't matter. Everett was safe.

She shifted her baby. He was heavy, even for the short distance to the exit. It didn't matter. She wasn't putting him down for anything, even as her hand shook from shock and Everett began to snuffle. She knew he felt her panic. Between that and the noise and the confusion of the last few minutes, she was surprised that he was as quiet as he was.

"It's all right," she whispered into his ear. She could smell the unique scent of the shampoo she'd used on his hair combined with the heavy smell of smoke. She ran a finger down his soft cheek, thumbing away the remaining tears. His bottom lip quivered and she knew that he was seconds away from bursting into a full-out wail. Once that happened, there'd be no stopping him. Everett's crying jags could be legendary. Now he had every reason to cry. She imagined that his flair for drama might mean she had a future actor on her hands. Or…she looked back at Talib, remembering.

She blew the thoughts from her mind. No matter Everett's discomfort or the former lover behind her, they could both wait. She needed to get her son out of this hotel and to safety.

And as she thought that a firm hand was on her waist and Everett plucked from her arms. Her heart stopped. This wouldn't happen again. She was ready to fight for her child. She turned and met the eyes of the man she had come here to see.

"Sara. He's heavy. Let me."

This time, his voice cut through her panic. His voice, like his presence, his personality, his everything, was too smooth and he was much too sure of himself. He looked the same and yet something had changed. She could see it in the depths of his dark, gold-flecked eyes. She couldn't put her finger on what it was, only that it was different, as if he was haunted by something or someone. A woman probably, she thought with scathing awareness and then pushed the thought from her mind. If she expected his help she would have to be civil and to do that she had to begin with her thoughts, and that one hadn't been fair. Whatever he was, he'd help her now. That was Talib, solid and dependable in anything that was not a romantic entanglement. Her mood dove again at that word. Entanglement. There could be no better or less flattering word for their failed relationship. And it didn't matter, for it was over—had been over for a very long time. It was another entanglement that was the problem, that was more than a problem, and that was why she was here.

He escorted her to the door, his hand holding her by the wrist as if he was her jailer. There was nothing she could do but be led to safety, to the place on the sidewalk that he deemed safe.

"Where are you taking us?" she asked.

He ignored her question. Instead he said, "You've spent enough time in this and the smoke can't be good for your little guy."

Her little guy. She sucked back relief. For coming here had been a risk. Finding Talib here today, more than lucky. Still, nothing could remove the fear. And she had so much fear. Fear for herself, for Everett, fear at facing Talib once again with the truth.

But despite all of that, she'd found him in the unlikeliest of situations. Not the most unlikely place. She'd known that he and Ian were friends, and that Ian had requested his help. That was the main reason that she'd chosen this hotel, it had been the timing that was strange. The bonus in all of it was that her travel agent had found a great promotion—everything had clicked together.

"Over here," Talib commanded and with those two words he made it clear that not only was he back in her life, but he was also taking charge, at least for now. And, at least for now, she would let him. Later—she hadn't thought that far.

This had been a journey of desperation. And now, despite having come all those miles to find him, she wanted to run—take her son with her before it was too late for both of them.

Instead she looked up at him. "I can't believe I ran into you in the midst of this. But I'm glad you were here to find—"

"What are you doing here, Sara?" He cut her off with a hint of anger in his voice.

The conceited donkey.

He thought she was here because of him. She looked at her son in his arms and that was the only reason she didn't lose it then and there. Unfortunately the truth of it was that what he was implying, what he'd left unsaid…he was right. She was here because of him, just for none of the reasons that the arrogant fool thought.

What she was here for was much more serious than any romance ever could be. And despite what he thought, and she knew very well what he thought, it was hard to deny the truth. He was a magnet for women, but he was no magnet to her. Not anymore. Those days were long over. But despite not needing him romantically, he was right about one thing. She did need him, she needed him very much.

For without him she was terribly afraid she was going to lose her son.

Chapter Four

Outside the hotel, Talib juggled the child in his arms as he put a hand on Sara's arm. It was an automatic gesture that rose out of the ashes of the past as if she'd never left, as if he'd never asked her to leave. It was strange how the truth of their relationship, how it had ended, had never been something he'd deceived himself about. He cared about her, but he couldn't be with her, not like that.

Sara owed him nothing, certainly no explanations. But the thought that she'd carried on with her life, married and had a baby, was oddly disconcerting. He pushed back the emotion, unable to face why it existed or what it meant. It was a moot point, he knew that. He had no right to question her actions and the sane thing to do now would be to push emotion to the background. Emotion did nothing in a situation like this. Still, it bothered him and it shouldn't. After all, he was the one who had broken up with her, gone his own way—forgotten about her. Or had he?

"Where's your husband?" he asked and wished he

could have rephrased. The question was more abrupt, more invasive even, than he had meant it to be.

"I'm not married," she said as she turned to look at him. There was defiance in her eyes—a defiance that had hooked him on a day that now seemed a combination of yesterday and so long ago.

"Oh, I…" he spluttered, unsure of what to say. He'd fallen into a gaffe of his own making and that was completely unlike him. But even now, she pushed buttons like no one else could.

"It's okay, say it. It's not like others haven't or at least thought it."

"Say what?"

"That you thought I was smarter than that. Smarter then becoming an unwed mother that…" Her voice choked off.

"Sara…" He stopped her with a touch of his hand on her shoulder. She'd always been, in some ways, unbelievably old-fashioned. "I'm not suggesting anything. We've been apart for a long time. What you do is none of my business. What is my business is getting you to a safe—"

"We'll go wait with the others," she interrupted and held out her arms to take her son.

"Just a minute. Wait," he said. It was odd how that need to protect drew him even now. He wasn't sure what Ian had planned for his guests, but for Sara and her son, he'd make sure they had alternate arrangements. He was on the phone for a little under a minute before he had things worked out to his satisfaction. The entire time he could feel her attention on him as he juggled the boy in one hand and the phone in the other.

"You're exhausted," he said as he slipped the phone into his pocket. "I've got another hotel arranged for you. Let me get you both safely on your way."

"But—"

"It was a long flight. Get some rest and then we'll talk."

"Thank you," she said softly. "But no."

She sounded in control, calm despite everything that had happened, yet her gaze seemed distracted, like it was all too much, and her face was pale.

"No arguments. It's on my account. You just take care of him, of the boy." He didn't tell her what he'd seen, why he was so concerned. He looked into her eyes. The look she gave him said that she trusted him and still he couldn't tell her that he'd saved her child from a potential kidnapping. He didn't know why she was here or what she wanted, but that need to protect, to not have her worry, was as alive as it had been during their relationship.

He put a hand on her shoulder. The fact that he knew the owner here, at the hotel they had only just left, was not a consideration. The hotel he was sending her to had housed royalty. It was secure on a whole other level.

"It's secure," he said as he pulled a pen and a business card from his pocket.

"I trust you," she said simply.

"I imagine you do."

"What is that supposed to mean?" she demanded.

"I'm not here because of you, if that's what you're thinking." But something about her voice sounded off.

"Yet, you're here in this hotel. My friend Ian's hotel. The one I was doing security for."

"I don't know what you're talking about." Again, there was that change in tone, as if she was telling him something that wasn't quite true.

"Don't you?" he asked, trying to tone down any sarcasm. "That all seems oddly coincidental."

Her lips tightened and she wouldn't look at him.

Everything about her was the same and yet so different. The child was the most glaring change. Having a child wasn't something she'd wanted, at least not when they were dating. He knew that because when they were together she had told him often enough how she was determined to make her career in management and one day open her own bed-and-breakfast. She'd been focused and had even said she'd have a family only when she was established. With no husband and with a child, and her longed-for career obviously in jeopardy, could this be about money? He'd never have believed that of Sara, that she'd looked him up so that he could support her in the lifestyle to which she wanted to get accustomed. It had happened before with other women, women he hadn't cared much about. It was always about the money, not about him—except maybe for the good time he showed them. But Sara, she was different.

"What are you thinking?" she said and that tone was in her voice, the one where she expected he was going to toe the line. But there was no line, no relationship. He looked at her, at her determined stance, and saw the stubbornness he remembered. Still, she'd changed. She had a baby.

She glared up at him. "You think I'm here because…"

"Because what, Sara?" he asked darkly. "You need help. You have a kid now. You need help and I—"

"You always could be a jerk," she muttered, cutting him off.

"Name calling, Sara?"

She looked at him with regret. "I'm sorry. That was beneath me."

He skated over her apology. It didn't matter. She could say what she wanted but he couldn't see any other reason for her being here. And the last thing they needed was to fight in a situation like this. It was unwarranted and it would upset the boy. "You'll be safer in the new hotel," he said, as if that ended the discussion. "Let's get moving."

Instead, she was silent, as if considering something, and then she looked up at him. "Tell me the truth, Talib. Did something happen back there in the hotel that you're not telling me? Besides the obvious—the explosion. I mean with Everett. It seems like you're not telling me something."

She was so bang on that he wanted to turn away from her. He wasn't sure what to say. So he took the safe path and said nothing.

"It's about Everett, isn't it? Where was he when you found him at the hotel? Did someone try to take him? Is that what you're not telling me?"

The tone in her voice, the words—all of it seemed to bring the heavy weight of responsibility. He wasn't sure why he would be feeling that for her, any more than he would for any other client. But she wasn't his client and there was the boy.

"No," he lied. He couldn't tell her the truth. He didn't know what the truth was. What he did know was that he could hear the edge of panic in her voice and she needed to be calm for her and for her son. Knowing wouldn't make a difference to her safety. He had taken care of that by arranging for the move. "I just want to make sure you're safe after everything that happened here. And the hotel you're going to has one of the best security systems in the city. Don't worry," he said, feeling rather low for lying to her the way he was. But in a way he felt justified for he knew she had yet to tell him why she was here and he wasn't completely convinced that money wasn't the problem.

"The security in this new hotel that you mentioned, it just frightens me that you think I need it. There's something you're not telling me, Talib." She looked at him. "But I'll let it go for now."

"I think that might be said for both of us. Here's my direct number." He handed her the business card he'd pulled out earlier—on it, he'd written the private number that few people, other than his family, had access to. "I'm available night or day at that number."

"Thank you, Talib," she said and despite the formality in her voice there was also something oddly intimate in her tone.

He hesitated. It wasn't a lover's caress that he remembered, or the stern, I'm-pissed-with-you tone. It was something else, something regretful, yet stronger than that. He'd consider it all later. For now, he had more important things to think about.

A car pulled up to the corner with one of his staffers driving. "Assad will take you there. The cost of the hotel is handled."

"Talib, no," she protested again.

"Yes," he said firmly. "I'll catch up with you later."

He opened the door and she slipped in, opening her arms for him to place her son in them. He couldn't turn away from the haunted look in her eyes and at the picture of the sleeping toddler in her arms. It was serene, so peaceful. This wasn't the Sara he remembered. This was so much more. He had to yank his thoughts back.

"Don't leave the hotel, Sara. Promise me," he said. "In fact, once you're in your suite, stay there. Order something to eat." He handed her another business card. "If you need anything else, use this number. He's a good friend and manages the hotel. Otherwise your money isn't good there…"

"Talib, no."

But her voice was quiet, resigned, as if she knew what he would say, where this was going.

"I'll be there later," he promised. This time his expression was serious as he handed her one more business card. "If you have any concerns at all and you can't reach me. Call my brother, Emir." He wanted to ask her so much more. Personal questions crowded with ones that might somehow affect this case. For now, he'd follow one of Nassar's cardinal rules—secure the innocent, regardless of whether or not they were potential witnesses.

"WE CAN'T FIGHT an Al-Nassar. As long as he didn't know, that was one thing. We could blindside him through Sara. Playing her was easy. But the Al-Nassars have resources. I don't know if they've ever lost a case." This wasn't turning out as Tad Rossi—who disliked his given name, Tadbir, and was never called anything but Tad—had planned. He knew he should have given this plan more thought, but when she'd run, he'd panicked. That wasn't what he'd intended.

"Speed will be our secret weapon."

"Secret weapon. You're talking stupid and—"

"Don't you ever call me that, ever!" The last word ended in a shout. "We clean house once and run," his partner said calmly as if he hadn't just lost his temper. "We'll be in and out before anyone is any wiser."

"What do you mean by that?" Tad gripped the phone. He was beginning to have qualms about contacting this man in the first place and definitely about calling him now. But he'd never expected Sara would run to Marrakech. And when she had, he'd become desperate. He couldn't lose her. He'd reached out to one of the few contacts he had left in that country and he'd known almost the minute he'd done it that it had been a mistake. He'd known him since public school. They'd been friends, as only two mismatched souls could be, and they had bonded together. He'd known Habib's disdain for the Al-Nassar family even then. He's also known that his childhood friend's life hadn't amounted to much except petty crime. Despite all that, they'd remained friends of sorts, oddballs thrown together by life. That was until he'd left Morocco. Then, he'd lost touch.

His old friend was someone who had every quality he required—ill feelings against the Al-Nassars and someone with no scruples. He hadn't anticipated that the grudge that motivated his accomplice was as large and far-reaching as it was. Unfortunately, now it was clear that the man would stop at nothing now that the window of opportunity had been opened. His ideas were outrageous and he couldn't believe what he was now suggesting.

"I know where he works and where he plays for the next few days. He's going to be tied to her and if he's not, he'll be at his friend's hotel. It's fairly easy, at least it is at the moment."

"Easy?" This had been a mistake and he was too far away to change any of it. "You have no idea what crap the Al-Nassars can pull, or the strings they've yanked. I wouldn't want to face one of them."

"Face? That's never going to happen." He chuckled. "That's the sweet spot. Talib Al-Nassar will never know who we are or who brought him down. He'll be done and never know what hit him. Besides, you screwed up, idiot. You're not even in the country. You've got no control over what happens."

He was right about that. Tad rubbed his thumb and forefinger together. He'd lost control and he needed to get it back. He needed to stop this thing, because what he was hearing was leading dangerously close to a place he didn't want to go—murder.

"The key to success is a clean sweep."

He knew what that meant. The only part of this plan that they both agreed on was the end, which left Sara as she had always been—a destitute single mother and of no interest to anyone, despite her model looks. That was exactly what she deserved. The only problem was that in his plan no one died. What was being proposed was nothing he would agree to. He needed to stop this before things got out of hand.

"It might only be about the money for you, but it's about much more for me." His accomplice continued, as if justifying his dark intent.

"That wasn't part of the deal."

"Too bad. But I see the biggest threat to my happiness on a morgue slab in the near future." Silence slipped darkly between them. "When that happens, money or not, I'll call it over."

He was insane. But Tad had known that before he'd contacted him. No, he corrected himself, he knew that he'd always been a little crazy. He hadn't expected this full-scale madness. He had to reel him in before his blood thirst destroyed everything. He'd acted on emotion, on panic, and reached out to the wrong man.

"This is over," he said. "I can't be part of this." He remembered how it had started, when he'd first seen Sara and been wowed by her looks. He'd only been into her for what he might get, then he'd thought it would be about sex but she'd disappointed there, refusing any of his overtures. It had been luck that had caused him to stumble on something even better than sex—money. When he'd realized who her son's father was he'd known he'd hit a gravy train he hadn't expected. That kind of luck was once in a lifetime.

"Too late. Dress rehearsal is over. We've taken the boy—"

"No!" Kidnapping wasn't in the cards—at least not what one would call a traditional kidnapping. A threat here or there, maybe. But murder hadn't been, either, and now he was suggesting both.

"You've lost control, my friend. It's my game now." He ended the call before Tad could say another word.

This was his fault, his stupidity. He'd bought time with a madman. He'd been desperate and desperate men did desperate things. He was living proof of that. But threatening to kill an Al-Nassar was insanity. Their reach and scope was not something a common man could go up against. He knew that, he'd always known that, just as he'd always known that it was Sara who was the key to everything.

And now it was Sara who was close to ruining his life, his plan—his everything. She was the path to getting what he wanted. He had to shut down his accomplice and he had to do it now. Except all he had was the twenty in his pocket. It wasn't enough for a bus across the country, never mind a plane across the Atlantic.

He was screwed unless he moved to Plan B. The thought of that cheered him, gave him hope.

If Sara wanted to play hardball, she'd be sorry. Soon she was going to learn who she was dealing with.

Chapter Five

Talib watched until the car was out of sight and Sara and the boy were out of the area—out of danger. He stood rocking on the balls of his feet, then spat the remains of his mint gum into the trash. He glanced at the No Parking sign above the trash can that was so faded, it was almost illegible. He thought of the boy. There was something familiar about him. In a way, it was like looking in a mirror. But that was ridiculous. Sara would never do that to him. She obviously liked Moroccan men and she'd made a mistake, but it hadn't been with him.

He reached into his pocket as if a pack of cigarettes was there. Stress always seemed to bring with it the need for tobacco. If nothing else, the gum took the edge off the craving and replaced a much worse habit that he'd kicked only six months ago. He'd started smoking three years ago despite his otherwise health-conscious lifestyle. It had been different then. He'd needed something, as the cliché went—a crutch. His mind flashed back to when Sara left. At the time, it seemed as though smoking was the only way to get through the pain he refused to admit he was feeling. Still refused to admit.

A senior police officer who he'd known for years came out of the north entrance, spotted him and came over. He gave the officer what information he knew.

Now, he waited as Ian crossed the street.

"How the hell could this have happened?" Ian asked, but didn't wait for an answer. "Anything new?" The frown lines carving his tanned face reflected his unspoken worry, that the explosion could have a catastrophic effect on a new opening.

"No," Talib said. "I haven't had a chance to do more than a cursory investigation and the police are still inside."

He had gone through the possibilities and checked the site before the authorities had arrived. "It all adds up to a fairly professional job, and yet, oddly amateur. I know those two images clash, but that's how it appears to have gone down. It seemed to be more a diversion than anything else."

He thought of the boy, Sara's child, that he'd snatched from the hands of a woman who claimed she was returning him. All that seemed a little much unless there was money involved. The Sara he knew had no money, but despite his assumptions, that all could have changed in the intervening years since they'd been a couple. He didn't know anything about her since their breakup. He'd been back to the States as part of his career with the family business on numerous occasions, and never had he looked her up. Mainly, he'd tried not to think about her. The end of their relationship hadn't been easy. It had been a blow to his pride, or at least that's what he told himself. The truth hurt a little too much.

He wasn't sure what to add to what he'd just said for he didn't know how the child and the maid fit in. "Of course, that's just off the top. I haven't had a chance to take a close look at the aftermath." The truth was that his thoughts couldn't focus.

Sara.

He couldn't believe she was here and he had no idea why she was. The last time he'd seen her had been in Wyoming. She'd been finishing up her last year of school and paying for it by working as a manager at the hotel where he was staying. Her appearance now was a mystery, one for which he didn't have an answer, and in the order of priorities, it would have to vie with the aftermath of the explosion and the investigation that would follow. He knew that the police would follow up with various hotel guests, but he'd pull a few strings to get her out of the fray. He'd do that because, no matter what had happened to the two of them, he still wanted to protect her. That meant making sure that neither she nor her son was any more involved than they needed to be.

"They seem to be petty thieves after money and jewelry. There was quite a bit of that taken," Ian said, breaking into his thoughts. "Three wallets and a purse are missing, but a jewelry bag in one of the suitcases holding some rather expensive jewelry was left. Odd, when it seems like a pickpocket was at work in the lobby, they miss a stash there for the taking."

One of the police officers spotted them and came over. "You were here at the outset?" he asked Talib.

"I was. I've given my report," Talib said. "Have you found anything else?"

"We've gotten all the physical evidence we can. Looks like the explosion was a diversionary ploy to commit a bit of petty theft."

"None of the rooms were disturbed. In fact, there's no evidence that the perpetrators went any farther than the main floor," he said, addressing Ian. "We'll be continuing with the investigation but we should be able to let you clean up the area later this afternoon."

"Seems a little excessive for petty theft," Talib said. He didn't like the direction this investigation was taking. It seemed slightly off-track.

"We've seen it before," the officer said, but his tone was almost defensive. He didn't give them a chance to reply but instead moved toward where the hotel guests gathered.

He was wrong, Talib thought. The explosion as a diversion for petty theft seemed too simple. In fact, it *was* too simple. It was why law enforcement in Marrakech had recently gotten a bad name. Too many crimes had been stuffed under the rug. But the police had their own problems with ongoing complaints of conspiracy and corruption. That aside, there was more at work here and the police officer either didn't know, or wasn't admitting to.

Talib thought of the scene with the maid and the boy. He'd told no one. He wasn't prepared to divulge what he knew. Not yet, and not to the authorities.

There had been too many recent issues with the police from the firing of a corrupt member, to the bungling of a recent tourist kidnapping. He wouldn't chance an error being made here. Far too much was at stake.

"We need to get your security one hundred percent in place, like I advised you weeks ago." There was an edge to his voice that only matched the darkness that seemed to fill his being.

"Talib?" Ian asked. "What's going on with you? It's got to do with her, Sara. I knew she'd booked but…"

"You didn't feel it necessary to tell me," Talib said. There was no question but only a slight recrimination in his tone.

"After three years, no. Man, you haven't been a couple for a long time."

"And it was none of my business."

"I suspected she had her reasons and if it had to do with you, she'd let you know." He looked at Talib with a frown. "What's up?"

"Nothing," he said. "I was just shocked to see her."

"Did she say why she's here?"

"No. And I doubt if it involves a need to see the country."

"My office," Ian said, and it wasn't a question. "We need to talk and it's the only place we'll get any privacy in this craziness."

Chapter Six

Talib nodded at the police officer who was monitoring the main doors to the hotel. He held up the distinctive card with its bronze-and-black flash of color that symbolized the Nassar company logo. The hotel was under lockdown but Nassar Security was well-known in Marrakech, almost as well-known as he was. Entering a scene like this was usually not an issue.

"I'm sorry." The police officer held up his hand.

"You're kidding me," Talib began with a scowl. "You won't let us back in?" This was unprecedented.

"Do you know who I am?" Ian interrupted.

"I don't care who you are," the police officer said. "No one's getting in."

"I own…"

"Get back before I have to use force." The police officer cut off Ian's words.

"I don't believe this." Ian shook his head.

Five minutes later they had worked their way through the emergency crews and around to a side entrance that wasn't being monitored.

"Back door?" the police detective asked with an

amused look as he met them a few feet from the entrance. He was in charge of the investigation and Talib had spoken to him earlier. In fact, he'd spoken to him in a number of instances on other cases in the past. He was one of the few Talib trusted. Now the officer greeted them with a frown.

"Overenthusiastic rookie wouldn't let us in," Talib said.

"I see." His grimace was half smile and half resignation. "Follow me."

"The explosive device was fairly unsophisticated," the detective confirmed five minutes later. "Looks to me like it was meant as no more than a diversion, to get what cash and jewelry they could." He looked at Talib, as if expecting that he'd provide some insight.

"Fortunately there were no injuries," Ian said. "Thanks for getting us in."

The detective gave them a brief nod. "All right, I'll leave you gentleman to it. If I can just ask that you stay away from the luggage area where the device was detonated, at least for now. They're still collecting evidence."

"This wasn't about me, was it?" Ian asked as the detective moved back into the room and into the heart of the investigation. "There's something you're not telling me."

"Get over yourself," Talib said with a smile that held an edge of dry humor.

He looked across the room. Suitcases lay scattered in the haze of smoke that hung lazily, as shadowed tendrils still drifted through the room. Talib and

Ian moved past the chaos and turned into a corridor, where Ian's office was separated from the main flow of the hotel lobby.

"My hotel is attacked—my guests terrified and probably not apt to come back to the Desert Sands and you want me to get over myself." Ian laughed, a dry mirthless sound that had more edge and no light-heartedness. "What happened to a little help from my friends or at least a little sympathy?"

Talib shook his head as Ian opened the door to his office. They entered a spacious, freshly painted office. New furnishings, complete with a large gleaming mahogany desk and black leather furniture, gave a solemn feel to the room. A vibrant painting full of color and reflecting the Atlas Mountains hung on the back wall and added a touch of color.

"Nice digs," Talib said in an attempt to be casual. In reality, it was the first opportunity that he'd had to see the finished office and what he considered the hub of his friend's hotel.

He sank into one of the leather chairs. He met his friend's worried look and knew the one person who needed to know everything was Ian. After all, the woman involved was in his employ. He began to tell him everything that had transpired. Ian was not just the owner of this hotel and a good friend—Ian Hendrik had once worked for Nassar. He'd been part of their research team before ending that career path to become an entrepreneur, beginning with the purchase of this hotel.

"So you think someone may have used the explosion as a smoke screen to kidnap the child?"

"Possibly," Talib said. "I'm not closing any doors right now."

"I'll find out the identity of the maid," Ian said. "Once we have that, maybe you'll have some answers."

"None of it makes sense."

"You're sure about that?" Ian asked.

"What are you suggesting?" Talib scowled.

"Someone tries to kidnap the child. I'd say they're trying to get money from Sara or her family."

"I considered that possibility. But unless things have changed, Sara has no money."

"Her family?"

"Same." He shrugged. "She doesn't come from money. The family fishing business has never been prosperous. It supports the family, her parents and her sisters' families, but that's about it." He looked off into the distance, as if he could find the answer there. "I had the office do a quick search on the family and on Sara. She's been underemployed for a while." He frowned—that information was not in line with the ambitious, professional woman he knew. Something rang sour about all of this.

"So the attempted snatching, just a crime of opportunity, black-market adoption?" Ian mused.

"I don't know." Talib shook his head. "Seems a bit of a stretch. I suppose we can only be thankful that the maid got cold feet."

"We've got a half-dozen children registered under the age of ten." Ian ran a hand through his hair.

"Frightening," Talib said. "We need to up your security, like yesterday." He didn't need to point out that his earlier advice hadn't been followed. That the hotel had opened under Ian's new management before all systems were in place.

"You were right," Ian agreed. "Whatever the reason behind this we can be thankful that no one was seriously injured. There was no irreparable damage done, except to my reputation. I'll reimburse any of the guests who lost belongings. Meanwhile, I've done a check with my public relations people. It looks like other than being shaken up, the hotel guests, with the exception of a few, are more than happy to take advantage of my offer. A free full-spa experience and one-night free stay, and coverage of alternate rooms for tonight. Most are willing to come back for the remainder of their stay here."

"That's generous," Talib said.

"You think? After scaring them to death with what looks like a terrorist attack." He stood up, pushing back from the desk. "It's the least I could do."

"Makes sense. You don't want to lose any business. Although, you're pretty much guaranteed to lose some."

"I don't think it will affect business in the long term and that's all that matters. That's my priority. That, and making sure that this doesn't happen again," he said with a look at Talib.

"When I'm finished, you'll have security that will

make the royal family jealous," Talib said. "This time give me carte blanche and stand aside."

"You're on," Ian said. "I can't have a repeat of this. I'll have my assistant get the employee records together. Should be an hour, two at most."

Talib glanced at his watch. "I'll check in with you later."

He stood up. His hand swept through his hair as if it was long enough to get in his face. Three years ago it had been. Three years ago he had experimented with a ponytail. Three years ago he'd experimented with a few things.

He left with a quick shake of hands and his mind already moving forward to the piece that didn't fit the puzzle—Sara and the boy.

Why were they here—why now… Why at all?

Chapter Seven

Sara shifted her sleeping son in her aching arms. She pushed back the soft dark curls that framed his face and repositioned him so that his weight lay across her, his head in the crook of her left arm. After Talib had given him back to her, in those moments of relief tinged with panic and despair, she'd seen what the future would be and she'd clung to her son. She would refuse to relinquish holding Everett to anyone, ever again. In the short time since Talib had found her, in all the chaos that had followed, he'd calmly made arrangements for an alternate place for her to stay and she hadn't been allowed to lift a finger. The arrangements had been made swiftly, silently and efficiently. She wasn't used to that. It was usually up to her, as a single parent, to do it all. Not now. The only thing she'd done was carry her son and she knew that she only had to ask and someone would do that, too. She wasn't ready to relinquish Everett after everything that had happened. She knew that after all the craziness of the explosion and evacuation, holding Everett was more for her than him. He was over it and she knew that as soon as he awoke, he would rather be on the ground, exploring on his own terms.

From the moment the car pulled up to the new hotel, the Sahara Sunset, again, everything was done for her. Assad opened the door. The valet offered to take her bags. She refused. She didn't have much. Her suitcase had been left behind at the Desert Sands Hotel, part of the evidence in the investigation.

Everett sniffed as if he was waking up and then settled against her shoulder with that familiar yet strange little sound. It almost sounded like an old man sighing. Sometimes her son seemed older than his years, and she wondered what he would be like as he grew up.

That thought made her more determined and her fright faded into the background as she entered the hotel lobby. Nothing could stop her. She'd come all this way. Now, the only challenge she had yet to face was herself. But she knew that fear could stop her despite the distance she traveled. One sign that Everett was safe without Talib's protection and she'd turn and run back the way she'd come. But that was asking for a miracle, and for the last seven months there had been none offered through the long days, transient jobs and three states. Every one of those days had been a nightmare, highlighted by fear that any minute she'd be discovered. Now, she had little money and no place to live. More importantly, no place to hide—no options.

She shifted her purse.

"Can I take that, ma'am?" a man with threads of

silver in his short, dark hair asked. He was wearing a djellaba with a gold belt around his waist. The traditional Moroccan garment had the insignia of the hotel on his shoulder. It seemed to be the uniform of many of the men employed by this hotel.

"No, I... Thank you. I have it," she replied. Even though that was a lie. She barely had it, one bag was slipping but she refused to relinquish any of her belongings. There wasn't much. Only her purse, the diaper bag and the bag with the essentials to get home or, alternatively, everything they would need if they had to run. It was an outrageous thought, but maybe not so much considering everything that had happened today.

She tried to stay focused and not be wowed by her surroundings, but it was impossible. Luxury enveloped her. The marble floors glinted across the massive lobby. The expanse of floor-to-ceiling glass circled the lobby and drew one's eye outside to the emerald green lawn and glimmering pool. There were elegantly uniformed staff everywhere. But they remained on the periphery, quietly available, slipping in to assist as needed. A massive chandelier sparkled overhead. It was only a decoration at this hour of the day, as sunlight streamed across the marble and reflected off the dark ebony trim of the registration desk.

This hotel was definitely out of her league. It felt like all eyes were on her and it was apparent that they knew of her arrival. It was also clear that she was going nowhere without someone three steps behind her. Talib's promise that she'd be safe had yet to be proven, but she was definitely feeling like she was well guarded.

She smiled and yet she felt more resigned than amused at the irony of staying in a place like this with her finances. She'd handed over the last of her retirement fund over three weeks ago and with nothing to meet Tad's demands, she'd run again. It was the fourth time she'd run; Tad had found her the other two. And on the third, she'd been in Chicago. That time, the message arrived by telephone before she could even secure a way to make a living. She'd gotten the cheap, throw-away phone to keep in touch with her family and to keep her number and location hidden from him. And two days after she'd gotten it, Tad had called in the dead of night, somehow having found her number.

The lavishness of the lobby made her want to bolt. The only thing that gave her any confidence was the fact that Talib had arranged this. Security and protection was his forte, she had no doubt that they'd be safe. But that was only part of the reason that she was here.

"Mama," Everett murmured in that sleepy, dreamtime voice. He was only shifting from one sleep level to another and was more than likely not waking up. The trip had been too long and too much for him. It had been too much for both of them.

"I'm here, baby," she whispered, humming the opening line of "My Favorite Things." It was the song her grandmother sang to her as a child, taken from

The Sound of Music. Her grandmother had sung it so many times to her. She'd sung it to Everett, in those first difficult months of being a new mother.

"Ma'am." A slim man about her age and dressed in a black, gold-trimmed suit, slightly different from the other employees, came over to her. "Can I help, a stroller for the baby, a—"

"No, thanks," she interrupted. She shifted Everett.

"Your room is ready. I'll show you to it."

Her room. Where would it be? How many floors up? Being higher up, farther from the street and possible danger, would make her feel safer. And yet, it was also more difficult to run to those same streets, to safety, should a threat lurk here, in this hotel. Hopefully it was high, but not too high.

Talib had said that they'd be safe. It was strange. After all this time and after everything that had happened, she believed him. He could keep her son safe. That knowledge had brought her across the ocean straight to him. But she knew she might have a better chance if she was upfront with him as quickly as possible. As things stood, he didn't know what she needed to be safe from. Could he protect the boy he didn't know from a threat that he didn't know about? She doubted it. She could only hope that what the hotel's security offered to its elite guests would be enough until she could tell Talib the truth. The truth she dreaded to reveal. The truth she had vowed to tell and the truth he so desperately needed to know.

She looked to her left, where a white-haired man stood lounging in a self-possessed kind of way. He was wearing an expensive-looking suit that had a look and cut that spoke of designer as opposed to off-the-rack. The look meshed with the confident way he stood, like he was used to being in charge. The woman beside him was at least twenty years younger. As Sara watched, she turned to speak briefly to one of the staff, who nodded and disappeared. As she turned back, the red sole of her Jimmy Choo stiletto was clear.

Those around her oozed wealth. They were people who lived lives that she could never imagine, opulent lives of privilege.

Her observations only served to make her feel even more out of place. She was sure that people were looking at her, at her simple, casual dress, like nothing anyone else in this lobby was wearing. She stood out. She didn't fit. She felt like a gold digger and yet she wasn't. This was about Everett, not about her.

Her thoughts shifted. She hadn't expected to find Talib so soon. What had he been doing at the same hotel where they had registered for their first three nights? And the explosion... The thought of it made her shudder. What did it all mean?

The only thing she knew for sure was what Talib had told her, that she and her son were safe here. That, she believed. It was words like that, that had her traveling across an ocean to a world that had once frightened her because all she could see were the differences. It was Talib's world, and it was this and other things that had driven them apart.

She was ushered into an elevator that was paneled in onyx. The walls were backlit so that the interior gleamed. This hotel was opulent in the extreme.

She shifted Everett and in the process hugged him tighter. He didn't complain. That was what she'd been afraid of, him sensing her tension. Instead, he was still sound asleep, exhausted. She was, too. Almost too tired to contemplate everything that had happened since they'd arrived. It had all been overwhelming and she needed Talib more than she'd even known. And she was frightened, more frightened than she'd been on the flight over.

She watched as the floors ticked away. Seventh floor, eighth. It was at the ninth that the elevator doors opened. The corridor was wider and more open than the standard hotel. There wasn't door after door, as there were in what she thought of as a normal hotel. They walked along a plush carpet edged in gleaming marble. Finally, they reached a door twice as wide as anything that she was accustomed to, and that shone from polish or just from the rich wood itself.

Inside, she was too overwhelmed to speak. Light flooded from a bank of windows in front of her. The ceiling soared at least twenty feet above her and the marble floor continued through the suite.

The bellhop showed her what was available and how to contact him. He took the most time going over the contents of a well-stocked bar, which, he assured her, had snacks appropriate for both her and her son. There was not just a minifridge, but a minikitchen set up to provide whatever she needed. Her mind flashed to Talib. She was both grateful and astonished that in the short time since her arrival, he'd made sure they had everything they needed. She noticed there was milk, juice and a small box of animal crackers—she had no idea where those could have been found, but they had.

As they finished the walk-through, she noted the large bathroom, the luxurious tub and the generous space so unlike any hotel room she'd ever stayed in. This wasn't a room but a small suite of rooms.

"Wait," she said as the man prepared to leave with a respectful bob in her direction. "I'll tip…"

He shook his head. "No, ma'am, you take care of the little one. The tip is handled."

"Handled?"

"Yes. If you need anything, you call me immediately." He bowed. "Sheik Talib Al-Nassar wants me to remind you that you are safe here. You are to order supper up and not worry about the cost. He will cover it. Stay in your room." He bowed again. "That is all."

He shut the door. She sank onto the soft leather couch, her son by her side. The opulence was lost in the feeling of despair she felt. Her son would be safe, but Everett would no longer be hers, he would be his, Talib's. Already, the process had started.

She closed her eyes. Everett was safe.

That was all that mattered.

TALIB HADN'T EXPECTED to be that long at the Desert Sands Hotel. But after going through the employee records with Ian, they were able to pinpoint one woman. Unfortunately, she was part-time and the address she listed turned out to belong to a cousin who hadn't seen her in weeks. Despite that glitch, he had one of the office staff tracking her.

It was dark, suppertime had come and gone. Hours had passed since he'd put Sara in the car with Assad. He hadn't had time to think of why she was here, and with a baby. None of it made sense to him, at least not the fact that she was here. She'd had a fear of traveling overseas. During the four months they'd been together and as his time in the States was waning, he'd half-jokingly said she should visit him here. She'd bluntly told him that that would never happen. She was quite comfortable never leaving the States or even Wyoming.

He stepped into the BMW, the earlier thrill of driving the incredible vehicle long gone. Around him Marrakech was lit up in its nighttime glory. It was a beautiful sight that inspired him every time he saw it. He never tired of it, yet tonight it didn't wow him as usual—he could have been anywhere. He could only think of Sara and why she was here, of what it might mean. Sara and the boy and the mystery of what had brought her to Marrakech. As well as the unlikely coincidence of finding her in that hotel in the midst of a catastrophic event. None of it added up. The hotel, he could get that. Ian had been running a blowout promotional sale that many of the tourist companies, as well as independent travelers, had picked up on. Sara undoubtedly realized she wasn't likely to get a better deal in the city, as far as location and convenience. That is, until the explosion.

In fact, he'd already checked. She'd gone through a travel agent, whose go-to hotel in the last two weeks had been the Desert Sands. There was a good chance that the hotel hadn't been picked by Sara, she'd only agreed on a choice. Her being there was more than likely coincidental. But the question was—why was she here in Morocco?

And why now? The more cynical side of him considered that it might be about the money. Why else? And yet that had never been Sara. But that was years ago. She had a kid now and he had no doubt that had impacted her career. She needed money and he had a lot of it. That fact had tempted more than one woman he'd known. They'd wanted him for superficial reasons, for the good time he could show them, for his unlimited resources. But Sara had never been the type to use people. She hadn't gone out with him for the money or the fine time he was capable of showing her. In fact, she'd begged off a number of times when he'd wanted to take her out for an exquisite dinner at an expensive restaurant. Instead she insisted on cooking for him at home, in her apartment. She'd refused to take anything but the smallest gifts from him, and even those she balked at. At the time, she'd seemed to truly be interested in him, in his company.

Was she capable of extortion or just plain begging for funds? Even if she was, she could have done that more easily than coming to Morocco. But that wasn't the Sara he knew. The Sara he knew had been hard-working—determined to learn everything she could about the hotel industry and eventually open the bed-

and-breakfast. She'd been passionate about that. But that was single Sara—unencumbered, sexually adventurous…fun. That wasn't the Sara he'd seen now.

This Sara had a son and her priorities had changed. He'd gotten the search results back on her. She hadn't held a job of any importance in quite a while. Something had radically changed. And the only one who had the answers was Sara.

It was time they talked about why she was really here.

Chapter Eight

When Sara opened the door, her gray eyes were sleep-clouded and Talib was brought back to another time, and another place. But she didn't smile when she saw him, nor did she look at him with eyes rich with passion. Those days were long gone. Instead, she frowned, and then, as if to compensate for not immediately welcoming him, offered him a shaky smile.

"Come in," she said quietly and stepped back. "The baby's sleeping," she warned. The way she said it gave the disconcerting and very real reminder that she was a woman who'd been at mothering for a while.

"How much do you need?" he asked as he moved into the room. He gazed at the boy sound asleep on the bed in the bedroom just ahead of him, his profile dimly lit by the soft glow of a nightlight, saw the impression where she had obviously just been lying beside him before he'd arrived. Probably asleep, too, he imagined. And at that thought, guilt ran through him at the blunt and potentially unfair question that he'd just thrown at her. He hadn't meant to do it, to say those words, at least not in that manner. He wished that he could pull them back, as he felt the unfamiliar bitter tang of remorse.

"What do you mean?" She frowned at him, her lips pursed, her eyes still clouded with the vestiges of sleep, and something else that he couldn't quite name.

"What are you suggesting?" Her voice was tight, contained, as if she was used to hiding her emotion.

He wasn't sure why he'd said it the way he had— raw, invasive, accusatory. But he knew that in doing so he'd opened Pandora's box and there was no going back.

"You haven't had a job in almost a year, not one of any worth, and you have a child. I can only assume you're broke and that's why you're here." They were fighting words and he couldn't stop himself.

"You..." Her voice shook and her face flushed, as it had in the past, when she was angry.

"I might not be in love with you, Sara, but I never stopped caring about you. How much do you need?" In fact, he'd wanted to compensate her when they'd broken up and he'd told her that. His brother, Zafir had later pointed out that offering money was pretty much the most insulting thing you could suggest to a woman. In fact, it was only then that he'd seen why she'd felt angry enough, that it justified scratching his car's paint with the heel of her shoe. She'd been furious and it had been weeks before he'd known exactly why. He had to admit that he'd grown a lot since then. Now he looked into eyes, which were deeper and so much older than they'd been three years ago, and waited for her reply.

Silence.

She'd traveled a long way but obviously lost her courage at the critical moment. He needed to step up and step in, and with that in mind, he offered her enough for her to live on and raise the baby, at least for a while.

Her lips tightened when she heard the generous sum he offered. He wasn't sure why—it was enough to keep her and the boy for the next five years in middle-class comfort. And plenty of time for her to get on her feet. He didn't think about all the reasons why he was so concerned about her, about another man's child.

"I…" She wrinkled her small, slightly freckled nose.

It was a habit he'd found both adorable and mildly annoying when they'd been together. He didn't like hesitation in anyone. Make up your mind and move forward. It was how he lived his life and what he demanded of others. The Sara he remembered had been a bit whimsical and, oddly enough, that had attracted him.

There were a lot of things going on here. He felt a twinge of guilt over the fact that someone had tried to take her son and she didn't know. The guilt was over the fact that he wasn't sure if he was going to mention it to her—at least not now, not right away. He wasn't sure what the motive was and he'd like to have more information before he told her. At this point he didn't know what had motivated the attempted snatching. For all he knew it might just have been a case of right age, right sex, right race. A chance to make money in the underground market, selling the child off to others desperate for a child of their own. He frowned at the idea.

The silence stretched between them.

"Where's his father?" He finally asked the burning question when she had yet to respond one way or the other to his offer. This was the question that had risen from the first moment he'd seen her and it was the question that circumstances had given him no chance to ask. Or the right, logic reminded him. But right or not, it didn't matter. He'd asked. It was out there, irretrievable.

"His father," she said and the words seemed to draw out as she backed away from him into the bedroom. There, she pulled a blanket over the boy and gently pulled his thumb out of his mouth. When she faced him in the doorway, her gray eyes were stormy as they locked with his. The connection broke swiftly as she looked away and back to her son, as if she couldn't bear to look at him for any length of time. But as he thought that, she whirled around to him, with her lips tight and her eyes sparking with a passion he couldn't identify.

"You tell me."

Chapter Nine

Sara took a mental step back, away from the anger building within her and that he'd-done-her-wrong feeling. She'd been baiting him and she had no right. It wasn't his fault that he had not participated in his son's life to date, that fell on her. But everything else was his fault. By default…

Sara yanked herself back from the pointless blame game. He wasn't psychic and yet she was treating him like he was. She should never have said what she had. She should never have set him up in a situation where he was clearly unable to defend himself. It hadn't been right and she knew she could do better. But she didn't have time to rectify any of it. They could only go on from this moment.

He'd always been insightful, slightly intuitive about everything, except, in the end, their relationship. Ironically, now, when he'd suggested that she was here for money—the thought grated, even though, for all the reasons he had yet to understand, it was true.

A knock on the door echoed sharply through the

room and made her jump. She stumbled against the couch and caught herself with one hand.

"Who is it?" Talib said in a voice that was more of a demand than a question. He moved toward the door as if there was a threat, as if he knew what she had yet to tell him.

Sara's heart pounded wildly—was there danger?

She gave herself a mental shake. She was seeing shadows and demons everywhere, but considering what had happened earlier, she was justified.

Even here they weren't safe. It had been proven. Unpredictable, undefinable things were threatening her everywhere and she wasn't sure why. Although the explosion must have been a horrible coincidence. She knew that. But so much had happened that she was seeing danger lurking everywhere. She had to quit it. She needed a clear mind to protect her son and she needed Talib. He was why she was here. No, she corrected herself, it was because of Tad that she was here, that she even needed Talib.

Tad?

Had he found her? That was an outrageous thought. There were thousands of miles separating them. She shivered. Impossible, she told herself. It was more than likely a hotel employee. And yet the shadow of him finding her hung around her like a cloaking veil. Her imagination kept taking her back to that possibility. The fear had followed her on the long flight across the Atlantic and it hadn't gone away since their arrival. Her heart beat wildly and her first instinct was to move back to the bed and put her body between whoever was at that door and her son.

She looked at Talib. He was physically intimidating, intelligent and a member of the powerful Al-Nassar family. They contracted to protect and their resources were astonishing and that was one of the reasons she was here. She had to trust him.

"Emir," Talib said as he opened the door.

Her heart seemed to skip a beat at the acknowledgement the fear could be set aside. It wasn't Tad.

Talib gestured his oldest brother inside, as if his arrival was expected.

"What are you doing here?" Talib asked as he looked back at Sara and seemed to almost deliberately place himself between her and Emir.

"I was in the area. I got your message, so rather than a phone call I thought I'd—"

"Right," Talib interrupted and it was clear from his tone that he didn't believe his brother's reason for being here.

Sara moved around Talib and put out her hand. "Sara Elliott. I used to—"

"Date Talib," he said with a smile. "I know. It was a poorly kept secret."

"No secret at all," Talib said defensively.

Sara looked at him with a frown. She'd never heard Talib speak like that. It made her wonder what he'd told his brother. But it didn't matter. She had bigger things to worry about than the fact that he might have fudged the truth of their relationship, possibly made it less than it was. But what had it been? She looked back to the bedroom door, to Everett. Definitely more than either of them had expected. She brought her attention quickly back to Emir.

"Nothing bad," Emir said with a smile. "In fact we thought for sure Talib was a goner." He looked laughingly over at his brother and received a weak smile in return.

Emir took her hand and shook it warmly. The expression in his eyes matched his handshake, as if he approved of her. Yet, that was impossible, he didn't know her. They'd never met. She was an ex, and she imagined in Emir's mind, immediately bad news. She couldn't imagine what he'd think when he knew about the baby.

Everett began to cry, breaking into her thoughts as he so often did. But this time he had her full attention, for he was beginning with that soft snuffle that would escalate into a full-scale demand if she didn't stop him now.

Emir turned and walked to the doorway of the bedroom.

"And who is this?" Emir asked, interrupting her instinctive thought to go to her son.

She didn't answer him immediately, as he seemed to not want an answer. Instead, Emir was focused completely on Everett's crying.

The nightlight glowed in the room as Emir went over to her son. He talked softly to the boy and seemed completely at ease with a cranky toddler.

She frowned. He was not like the man she'd heard of in stories that Talib had told her. In those stories he had been almost legendary. There was something softer about him. Maybe love did that. She'd heard that there was love in the air between him and one of the Wyoming agents. She'd also heard that a marriage was planned. She wasn't sure if that was what had changed the man Talib had described, or if his perception of his brother was different from what hers might be. Whatever it was, it didn't matter. She didn't need Emir guessing what she had yet to tell Talib. That would only make a bad situation so much worse. But there was no stopping him. For a moment Sara's heart seemed to stop. *Please, no*, she thought. *Just give me this one break and I'll tell him.* Seconds felt like minutes as she waited for Emir to blurt out what, to her, seemed so glaringly obvious.

"You don't mind if I pick him up?" Emir smiled at her over his shoulder. "Good practice for me. Not that we have any children yet but Kate and I both…" He shrugged. "Someday."

She blew out a quiet breath as Everett smiled at him and actually chuckled when he picked him up.

"You might as well bring him out where we are. He's not going back to sleep for a while," she said as she turned and left the room. She glanced over her shoulder to see Emir following her with Everett in his arms. It was strange and the odd thought hit her that Emir, under different circumstances, could easily be a favorite uncle.

"You need a wedding first," Talib said interrupting her thoughts and Sara inwardly cringed at the words.

First comes love, then comes marriage… It was

an old saying, but it was one that underlined the values she'd grown up with. The values that she'd found herself so far on the other side of. It was why she hadn't gone back to her family for help. While they wouldn't turn her away, their disapproval would be a dark shadow to raise Everett under. She wouldn't do that, because it would mark the man he would eventually become. She hoped eventually that her family would come around, become more open-minded. Now, it didn't matter. Since she'd run, she had kept in touch with them via private messaging on social media. Because, no matter what their feelings were about the situation, they'd come to accept it. Ironically, in the past months of long-distance communication, it was clear that while they might not like that their daughter had given birth to their grandson as a single woman, in the end they loved both she and Everett and, because of that, they worried.

"He's good with kids," Talib told her. "Most likely because he's the oldest."

Sara was at a loss, grateful for the size of the room, because in a normal-size hotel room these two vibrant Al-Nassar brothers would have overwhelmed her. Power seemed to emanate from them. It was a self-assuredness that she would like to have said was more pronounced with Talib, but that wasn't the case. They wielded their authority with ease, but in different ways. Even here, Emir was larger than life and Talib even larger than that, at least physically. She sank down on the bed as Emir handed her son back to her. But the look Emir gave her was like the moment of truth. She could see it all in his eyes. He knew the truth that had yet to be told.

The hand that he put on her shoulder, as brief as it was, spoke of support and solidarity. As she met Emir's ebony eyes, she sensed he knew. He had seen the truth in her son's face. Even he couldn't help but see how closely the boy resembled Talib.

Talib had the power to take her son and offer him the life she could not. Running from the blackmail rather than turning to Talib had been a bad decision. It wasn't until she'd run out of places to go that she'd been willing to turn to the one man that could help her: Talib. But seeing Emir and Talib together terrified her because it reminded her of everything she stood to lose. Everett was one of them in a way she never could be. The Al-Nassar family had the power and the might to run roughshod over someone like her. They had the resources to claim Everett and raise him as their own. And the head of all that might was making this room just a little too crowded.

The nightmares that had awoken her so many nights in a cold sweat, trembling with what she imagined the future could be, seemed so much closer to becoming a reality. Emir had squeezed her shoulder, as if telling her he was on her side, not to worry. Or maybe all of that was wishful thinking. It would be nice to have one member of the family on her side. But was he on her side? The Al-Nassar brothers' loyalty to each other and their sister ran deep. But the look that was now on his face confirmed not only what she already suspected, but that he also guessed that Talib did not know.

"The hotel's secure?" Emir asked as he turned to Talib.

"It is."

"I heard there was an explosion…"

"Handled," Talib said shortly. "Look. Can we talk later?"

"There's a case I want you to take." Emir looked at his phone as it beeped a message. "Take care of whatever you need to, tonight. And I'll brief you in the morning. If you're not needed here…" He let the words trail off, but his eyes were on her and not Talib as he nodded and exited the suite.

"What was that about?" Talib asked as he came over to her. "I thought you'd never met Emir."

"I didn't."

"Then what was with the look between the two of you?"

"Sit down," she said, indicating the bed, where Everett had again fallen asleep.

She'd run out of time. But this wasn't how she'd meant to tell him.

He didn't sit down; instead he strode away from her. He stood distant and alone, looking out at the night sky of Marrakech. A minute passed, then another.

She stood up and followed him into the sitting area where she stood for a moment, watching him, as she contemplated what she needed to say. She took a breath. She'd wasted enough time.

"When we broke up..." *I was devastated*, she thought. *And you couldn't have cared less.* Instead she said, "A few weeks later, I..."

He turned from the window. His emotions were hidden in the unreadable look that had frustrated her so much throughout the span of the last few days of summer that led to the breakup. Before that, it had been a magical time.

This was so hard.

"I'm sorry about your car," she said, thinking of how she'd deliberately scratched the paint with the heel of her shoe. It had been so long ago and yet she'd been sorry about it ever since.

"My car?"

He frowned and something in the way his brows drew together reminded her so very much of Everett. Who was she kidding? Everything about him reminded her of Everett.

"Never mind." She shook her head. "It's irrelevant." She felt stupid having said it, but it had been one of those involuntary things that you just spit out and regret later. The car was now long gone, or at least she assumed so, and would have been replaced by a newer, more exquisitely expensive sports model. That was Talib. Some things never changed. She twisted her hands together and considered how to begin even though she'd gone over this a dozen times.

"You came to see me," Talib said quietly, as if encouraging her to continue.

She wasn't ready. She turned the words around in her head.

"In Wyoming, you never wanted to break up. I regret all of it now, at least how it ended. I didn't want you to leave that way. I should have known how you felt, I should have…" He broke off as if gathering his thoughts. "It was me and…"

Her jaw tightened.

"Things have changed, Sara, but I'm still the man you remember, I…"

His words were a low rumble in the back of her thoughts as her disbelief seemed to mute the sound of his voice. What was he talking about? He couldn't possibly believe that she'd come here to beg to be back in his life? He couldn't possibly. But he'd always been an arrogant son of…

There was no time for such thoughts. She combed her hair with splayed fingers, then dropped her hand. She had no defense. He was right. She had come to see him and as difficult as it was, she had to remember why she was here. Tell him, the voice of reason inside of her screamed. And then figure out how to tell him why she'd hidden this from him for so long.

"Everett…" she began.

She couldn't do it.

Her next words were going to change everything, and the neat little life she had built would crumple around her. Who was she kidding? The neat little life had been blasted into oblivion by one stupid move months ago. One date that turned into a half dozen with the wrong man. Now she was in a corner and there was nothing she could do, other than the one thing that would protect her son. The one thing that would destroy the world she had still hoped she could return to.

His eyes seemed to hold shadows, as if he felt her pain, as if he knew. She saw the promise of courage and strength that mirrored the passion he lived by. They were eyes she could drown in if she didn't stay strong.

She took a breath. She'd flown halfway around the world. She'd dodged a madman for months and arrived here in desperation, willing to lose what she loved most in exchange for the promise of his safety. There was no more delaying.

She met his scrutiny, and it seemed to hit somewhere deep inside of her. She didn't have time to wait for courage and she no longer had an excuse for keeping it secret. She'd determined that when she'd bought the plane ticket for Morocco.

The truth needed to be told. It couldn't wait another minute longer.

She looked up, met his gaze and with all the courage she had—held it.

"Everett is your son." She blurted out the words before her doubts took over once again.

This time the silence hung heavy in the room.

"My son," he finally said.

"Yes," she whispered. "Everett Talib." She said his full name, as if that confirmed everything. And in a way it did. The second name referenced the fact that Everett belonged to the Al-Nassar family. One day she'd fully intended that he would know his father and claim the heritage that was his right. But one day wasn't supposed to be until Everett was older. One day was when he was able to make his own decisions. When he was safe from being ripped out of her arms by a man who had more power than she could ever imagine.

Circumstances had worked against her.

"And you thought now was a good time to tell me," Talib said, turning a question into a statement, and the statement into an accusation.

The moment that followed seemed to tick like a retro alarm clock between them. The silence was full of recrimination on his part, and fear on hers. He didn't look at her but instead walked away and stared out the window before turning again to face her.

"Why, Sara? Why now? Two, three, if you count pregnancy, years later." His voice was low, in that way of his when anger was brewing just below the surface.

She didn't say anything. Seconds ticked by and turned into a minute.

"And why would I believe you? How can I believe that there weren't other men, that…" He ran the palm of his hand across his chin and his gaze never quite met hers.

She was shocked. He'd actually insinuated that not only had there been other men, but that there also might have been many men. There'd been Tad, but that had never been physical. She couldn't, not after… Her thought dropped off. Somehow, of all his possible reactions, she'd never thought that he wouldn't believe her, that he would think so little of her. "I don't expect—"

"Don't say anything, Sara, please." He swung around. "I've sensed from the moment you arrived that money was the issue. I didn't want to believe it. That was never you."

She should be angry. She should tell him where to go, but shock and desperation seemed to act as a wet blanket to any outrage she might have felt.

Instead, she wanted to deny his accusations. She wasn't a gold digger. She'd starve first, but that was herself she was talking about, not Everett. Her stomach clenched. Now, to admit the truth was to admit that he was right, it was about money. For it was only money that could save her son.

"So, why now, Sara? Did you think this was adequate punishment for the breakup?" He shook his head. "Keeping my son from me. That is, if he is my son."

"He is," she said. "Look at him." For it was true. Everett was his father's son. He had skipped over her fair complexion, gray eyes and light brown hair streaked with blond. Instead, he had his father's thick, black wildly curly hair, although in the sun it was a softer curl that framed his olive-toned face. If he was awake, you could see the warm eyes that had so many times reminded her of the man she'd loved and left. Or, more specifically, asked her to leave. And if he looked at his hands, he would see that even as a baby, Everett had extremely long fingers, like his father. "I meant to tell you eventually. Just not now, but—"

"Do you have a birth certificate?" he said, cutting her off in a voice that had a dark edge.

"You're not on it," she admitted softly and this time she couldn't look at him. It was an admission that had been a long time coming and one that drove the final nail into her betrayal. But he was his son and he needed his father and it was that fact that had her standing her ground.

Silence beat accusing wings around them.

He'd stood with his back to her, now he turned to face her.

"We left on bad terms, Sara, but I never thought you'd do this, keep—"

"Is that what you think?" she interrupted, struggling to keep her voice low, so as not to awaken Everett. "That I kept your son from you so that I could punish you? You arrogant son of a donkey," she whispered. This conversation had to end. It was not something to discuss around a baby, sleeping or otherwise.

"I can't believe this," he said. "My son," he mused, as if saying the words made them more palatable.

A minute passed, as if he needed the time to absorb it all.

There were things she wanted to say and she said none of them. Instead, her bottom lip quivered and she knew that she had to tell him everything and soon, before it was too late.

Chapter Ten

Talib ran a hand along the back of his neck, like he was too hot, but the only thing hot was the situation. He stood there for a minute, maybe two. Neither of them said anything. It seemed like there was so much to say and yet all of it ran too deep.

"I'm sorry, Sara. I know I'm not dealing well with this. I…" He shook his head. "I'm not sure what to say. I believe you, he's my son and I'll do right by him, but I need some time."

She looked at him with a frown. "There's more I need to tell you. Everett—"

"Not now," he said shortly. He knew she'd heard the edge in his voice. He could see that in her face. He couldn't help that. It was all too much. He was overwhelmed. He needed time alone to figure out what he felt, but the doubt wasn't about the boy or about being a father to him. That was a given. It was about the lost time, about Sara and her deception.

"Keep the door locked. You're safe here. Despite that, don't open it for anyone. I'll be back."

"When? This is important. I—"

"Tonight," he interrupted. "The hotel is secure. You'll be safe. But for now, stay in your suite."

She frowned.

The door of the suite shut with a finality behind him. It made him remember that other door shutting almost three years ago. Only then the door had slammed, brutally closing in conjunction with words that told him where to go. In a way it had been like their relationship, high-powered and unpredictable. And yet, he'd never forgotten her.

It was all too much and he was furious with Sara. Whatever her reasons, one more minute in that room would have had him doing something juvenile like put a fist through a plaster wall. It was a thought that in real life he doubted would give one any satisfaction. But the fact that the thought was there had frightened him. What he needed was time and space before he said something to her that no apology would ever repair.

His heart pounded and he wasn't sure what he wanted or needed to do. He wasn't thinking logically. The familiarity that had immediately struck him between Everett and himself… He had blown off believing that Sara would never deceive him about something that important. Now, the truth of her deception took his breath away. He only knew that he needed to get out of the confines of the hotel and get some air.

He'd been deceived on a scale that was unfathomable, by a woman who he thought incapable of such a thing. He clenched his fist and his jaw twitched.

He pushed past the uniformed bellhop and past another man, who looked at him oddly. He needed to get it together, but first he had to get his emotions under control.

If it was true, that this boy was his son, he'd missed so much. He wasn't sure what it all meant or how this could have happened. They'd used birth control. They'd been careful, but obviously not careful enough. It didn't seem possible and yet he knew she hadn't lied. He strode through the lobby, heading through a side door and into the parking lot.

"Why now, Sara? Why the hell now?"

It had worked beautifully and still it had failed. Tad Rossi rubbed his thumb against his index finger. His teeth were clenched and his back molar ached. He'd have to get that fixed one day. Except that he had no money even for emergency dentistry. He'd maxed out what little credit he had and borrowed everything he could from what little family he had. But they'd long since closed the door on him. He'd been scrounging ever since—living off his good looks and the back of one girl or another.

He needed to get to Morocco and he needed to get there without delay. But he had no resources, that had been the reason behind all of this. Sara had been a lucky find. The fact that she was hot enough for any man—a bonus. She was nothing now. He'd drained her of everything, at least everything monetary, or so he'd thought. Then, she'd surprised him. Getting more money out of her should have been easy. She should have done what he asked and she had, and then she'd stopped.

"Damn," he snarled. The plan was now far bigger than terrorizing one resource-limited woman. Al-Nassar had money, more money than he wanted to contemplate. But that had been his first mistake—sharing that part of the plan. He'd set something in motion that he wasn't sure he'd be able to stop, at least from here.

Sara and the boy were nothing. Neither of them mattered. Despite his initial interest in her, like any woman, that hadn't lasted long. Sara had been pleasant enough and the child mattered not at all. Although he'd threatened kidnapping to encourage her to get more money, he didn't want the child for any longer than it took to get his mother to comply.

He couldn't believe she'd run. That had been a major oversight on his part. She'd run before, that was true, but it was also true that it had been in the United States. She'd been easy to find. A computer-geek friend, an app that easily fished information out of a social-media site and he was in business. The bonus was that she was conscientious about contacting her parents through social media. In a private message to them, she'd left a contact number each time. He'd followed that trail with ease. But Morocco was another story.

He was losing his touch. He couldn't believe that this had happened, that he'd read her wrong. She wouldn't have chanced it if she wasn't desperate. He'd pushed her too hard.

He remembered the moment like it was yesterday. He'd picked up his phone and punched a number that had been on his contact list for over a decade, spoken with someone he hadn't in years. But it was a man whom he'd always felt was a kindred spirit.

When the call had ended, they'd reached an agreement. One that hadn't made him happy, for it had been no agreement at all, only demands. He had to fix what he'd put into motion before he screwed himself out of the money that was his. He needed to get to Morocco and take control of his own scheme, but to do that he needed money.

Everything would have been fine, if he'd kept a level head. But it had felt like his world was falling apart. He panicked, unable to think of how he would come up with the funds to even purchase an airline ticket to get there and get control of his own game. He'd been desperate. It was the quick rip-off of an elderly woman at an auto teller that had been his next mistake. He hadn't expected the woman to not only fight and knock him off balance with a kick to the shins, but also yank out a shrill whistle and blow it again and again.

He'd turned to push her out of the way, but she still had the whistle. When he'd decided to give up and run, he'd been waylaid by a punch from an overexcited do-gooder.

And all of it ended in a humiliating choke hold as the curtain fell on his plan. Instead, the plan was radically changed by the glaring flash of the lights of a police cruiser. The memory of being roughly frisked and read his rights and then a forceful hand on his head that shoved him into the dark interior of a police cruiser.

Now there was no stopping the force of the Pandora's box he'd opened.

For him it was over, for Sara...it soon would be.

Chapter Eleven

It felt like the breath had been knocked out of him. Talib had never imagined what it would feel like to learn that he was a father. He only knew that this wasn't how it was supposed to be. This wasn't how most people might feel to become a parent. But most people didn't become a parent in this manner. In a way he felt robbed. And what he knew for sure was that he was feeling too much. He needed to get it together and figure out this mess. He had to shove the emotions into boxes that they just didn't want to squeeze into. He hated the feel of this, of being over-whelmed with confusing feelings for another human being.

That had only happened once before. It had been Sara who had precipitated that confusing melee of feelings as well, but that time it had been in a good way. In the first blush of new love, in the hot de-mands and passion of a series of firsts. He'd broken up with her when the need for her had become too much, when it was all he could think of. But she'd gotten one up on him. She'd taken his son with her. He wasn't sure if he could ever forgive her for that.

"Damn!" He smacked his fist into the palm of his hand.

Only his parents' deaths had made him feel anywhere close to this betrayed. And their demise hadn't been accidental—it had been murder. The emotion he felt now was different, but just as intense.

He stood at the door to her hotel room for a full five minutes before he could bring himself to knock.

When she opened the door less than an hour after he'd left, neither of them said anything. Instead, he looked beyond her to the bedroom where the boy slept, but there was only a small hill beneath a blanket in the middle of the bed. The outline of the child was there and now, instead of the nightlight, a small bedside light was on so that the boy wasn't in the dark. The living area was dimly lit by one lamp on a desk and the blush of city light coming in from a window where the blind was partly up.

"I expected more of you than that," he said as he strode past her.

Seconds ticked by and the silence deepened.

"You expected…" She said the words softly, as if she couldn't quite fathom the meaning of what he was trying to say. "More of me? I wanted more of our relationship. I expected more."

"You could have told me. I would—"

"If you couldn't handle our relationship, how were you going to handle a baby?" she interrupted.

Silence pulsed through the room.

"Why are you here, Sara? Why now?"

"I never wanted you to know," she said. "At least not now. Not while he's so young."

The words were like a razor slicing skin. It hurt like few things could. He knew the boy was his son. He didn't think she'd lie about that. He'd seen the similarity as much as he'd wanted to discount it. It was what she had done, or more accurately, what she hadn't done that bothered him most of all.

"You had no right," he said through clenched teeth.

"Didn't I?" She paused. "You were the one who walked out on me, not the other way around. Would you have come running back if I'd told you?" She turned away.

That she thought he would walk from such an epic responsibility was inconceivable. He wanted to shout at the injustice of it all, but the source of his upset was sleeping not that far away from them.

Silence ticked between them as she waited and he fought for control.

He couldn't look at her. Instead he turned his back to her and to the view of Marrakech, the city he knew so well and, in this moment, couldn't care less about. He wasn't sure who he was angry at—her, himself, or fate. Her words were valid. Three years ago, he hadn't been ready for a relationship. But a child, that was different.

Minutes passed.

He went over to her and stood just behind her, hesitant to come any closer.

She slipped past him, moving back into the living area.

He followed her.

"I wanted him to see where his ancestors came from," she finally said.

"At two?"

"It's never too soon," she said.

"You're not the adventurous type, Sara. Travel wasn't your thing and definitely not with a toddler." He came over to where she stood, looking small and vulnerable, one shoulder against the wall. She wouldn't look at him. He needed her to look at him. He put a thumb under her chin, nudging her to look.

"What's going on, Sara?"

But his gut already knew. It was about money, like he'd already so ungraciously said. Her evasive nonanswer had been answer enough. Even though that was so unlike her. Even though he would have said with some assuredness that never would such a thing happen, now it was the only explanation that made any sense. All of it, her being here with the boy, at the hotel that he, at the moment, had a vested interest in—all of it stunk of desperation.

"Damn it, Sara," he said with a sharp edge that seemed to knife through the room.

She shook her head and a tear rolled down her cheek.

"I'm desperate or I wouldn't be here." She met his gaze with a half smile that was no smile at all. "I'm being blackmailed," she said bluntly. "My ex-boyfriend. We didn't go out long and we never…"

She shook her head. "Never mind. That's none of your business." She was quiet for a minute, collecting her thoughts. "He didn't like Everett. Actually, that's not true, he just didn't want anything to do with him. Because of that, I broke things off. Actually, it was because of a lot of things."

A minute passed, then two.

"It turned out that he wasn't interested in me. But he was interested in any money I could give him," she added and a sour thread ran through the words.

"A man leaching off a woman," Talib said with disdain. There was nothing wrong with a strong, independent woman. That had been Sara. But there was everything wrong with a man who couldn't support himself.

"He was a stockbroker, at least that's what he said." She paused and wiped the corner of her eye. "It wasn't true. He was only a two-bit con man who gambled his money away in the stock market."

She looked at him with wide eyes, a look that would have had her in his arms all those years ago. Instead he stood there and waited, prepared to wait for as long as it took for her to tell him the truth, all of it.

"He went through my things one day when I was in another room changing Everett. I'd written out a list of instructions, in case anything happened to me. I wanted Everett to know who he was, where he came from. He saw your name." Her eyes met his. "And your family, what I know of them. He saw it and…" She bit her lip, her fingers lacing through each other. "He knew who you were."

"How?"

She shook her head. "I don't know. He was Moroccan, but… I don't know how he knew who you were or, more importantly, that you had money."

"And he's the one who blackmailed you?"

"He threatened to tell you…about Everett." Pain seemed to lace each word, as if saying the fact again was more difficult than the first time she'd said it.

"What was his name?"

"Tad Rossi." The name was stilted, without inflection. She folded her arms across her chest and turned away.

She was silent, and he waited. This was on her. Her regret, her mistake.

He waited until she turned around again to face him, but the pain in her eyes broke his resolve.

"I could have protected him, and you."

"I know," she whispered.

"You should have told me," he said and he couldn't filter the anger from his voice. "If I'd known from the beginning, nothing like this would have happened."

"I was afraid," she said softly. She'd moved to the couch, flopping down as if her legs would no longer hold her. "You're my last resort. I've given him all the money I can. Now, if I don't give him all the money he's demanding." She shook her head. "I don't know how this is going to end. I'm scared that he might take Everett exactly like he threatened."

"Over my dead body," he snarled. "That will never happen."

"They've found me everywhere I've gone." Her

cheeks were flushed and her eyes were filled with pain. "I've moved to three different states in the last seven months."

His fist clenched at the thought of her running, frightened and without resources.

"Everett in his hands for even an hour is incomprehensible." Her voice trembled.

Never. Not while I still live, he thought. And as far as the creep that had been stalking his girl, he would put an end to that. The thought stopped him—Sara was not his girl, not anymore. Then he remembered something else she had said, maybe just a misplaced pronoun, maybe something more.

"You said *they*. Who else is there, Sara?"

"I don't know if there's anyone else. It's intuition only," she said. "What I know of him. Some of the things he's done are out of character. It's like he's getting advice somewhere else. And at the Desert Sands Hotel—I almost felt like whoever it was, whoever was helping him, was there. But that's crazy and there's no reason to believe anything like that. He didn't have the resources to travel. He gambled away everything he had."

"From what you've said, it's been a while since you've seen him. What resources he might have now is pure speculation. He could have found what was needed to come here, to follow you."

"Talib, you're frightening me."

"How are you contacting your family?"

"Through social media messaging."

He grimaced at that.

"What? I… I don't tell them much. Give them the new mobile number to reach me. It's safe, it's…"

"There are apps that can hack that without problem, Sara," he said. "I'm not saying that's how he found you, but that's definitely one way."

She shook her head. "I can't believe it. I used disposable phones so they couldn't get to me. The numbers are changed out regularly." She frowned. "I messaged my parents with the new number every time."

"On social media. That wasn't the smartest move."

Their research team had recently briefed him on another case, showing him how information could be mined from the web. One of the easiest places to fish for information was through social networks and their messaging systems.

"I…" Her words choked off. She was clearly overwhelmed as she realized the mistake she'd made. She had chosen to avoid calling her parents because she wasn't ready to answer the questions they would ask or the demands to come home that they'd already made. Both had been more easily evaded in writing than by telephone.

In another time and in another place, he might have apologized. Not now. She needed to be on guard. His gaze went to the bedroom—there was too much at stake.

He thought of the scene in the first hotel, the maid holding his son, her claim that she had been paid to bring him to a man who waited somewhere outside. He thought of how close he'd come to losing his son before he'd ever gotten a chance to know him, and the thought of that was incomprehensible.

"I can't lose him," she repeated. "I'll pay you back, Talib. I promise. If it takes me my entire life."

She would never pay him back. He wouldn't allow it. But he told her none of that. Instead he asked, "How much, Sara? How much do you want from me?"

She flinched and he knew that it was because of the way he'd worded that last question. He felt like the biggest jerk, the biggest bully. He'd worded it that way to make her feel uncomfortable. But now, seeing her discomfort, it didn't give him any pleasure. In fact, looking at her, he was afraid he'd broken her.

He was relieved when she drew her shoulders back and looked at him with stoic eyes. Even though her lips still quivered, she was giving him attitude, backbone—she was far from broken.

And then she told him what she needed.

At first he didn't know what to say. The figure she mentioned was large even by Al-Nassar standards.

"We'll get this fixed. He won't get away with this and you don't need to worry, Sara. Not anymore. I'll handle whatever demands they have directly." No matter what she had done and how she had deceived him, Sara and his son would have no worries from here on out.

His fists clenched as he paced the room.

There were questions that needed to be answered, two years to catch up on and so much more that he hadn't addressed. But in truth, he couldn't look at her or his son another moment. For she only reminded him of the deception and the sleeping child reminded him of all that he had missed. He needed time and space, they both did. The morning would come soon enough.

"Get some sleep," he said. "I'll be next door."

SARA'S PHONE RANG at exactly 3:15 a.m.

Her heart stopped.

This was the time when all the calls had come in. It was the exact time that Everett had been born. She'd forgotten to tell that important fact to Talib, but their conversation had been so overwhelming.

She debated not answering, but she didn't want to wake Everett and she knew that he'd call again and again, until she answered. They would not give up. She'd purchased a disposable phone again, as she had every time she'd run. And he'd found her again, as he had every time. It was like a never-ending story that one might read to a child before bedtime, except this story threatened a very bad ending. She remembered what Talib had said, about the app that could track her and she cringed.

She pushed Talk with a shaking finger.

She didn't say anything. She couldn't bear to say more than necessary. Just to think that this man had once kissed her, that she'd allowed certain liberties— all of that made her queasy. The only good thing that hadn't happened, consummating it—she would always be thankful he had never been the man in her bed. The thought of that made her want to hurl.

"He can't protect you," a snide, almost robotic voice said.

"Who are you?" She frowned. This wasn't Tad. Not only was it not his voice, but Tad wouldn't play such games. He would speak to her directly, as he always had.

"Next time we'll take the boy and he won't be able to stop it."

"What are you saying?" And who is *we*? she thought.

"You don't know?" A dry chuckle followed—it was more creepy than humorous. "If not for your boyfriend, we would have taken the kid before the fire was out at the Desert Sands."

"What?" Her breath caught in her throat.

"Preventing that kidnapping was only luck on his part. Next time it will be real. Nothing except money will stop the inevitable."

The call broke off and Sara dropped the phone like it contained poison that might seep into her skin.

Her mind went back to the hotel, to the smoke, the panic at losing Everett. It had been Talib who had found him, maybe even saved him, but saved him from what? Was the caller just playing with her emotions or had something happened that Talib had failed to tell her?

She looked at her watch. Fifteen minutes had gone by.

She couldn't believe that Talib hadn't told her that her son had almost been taken. It was typical Talib, the need to protect, to shelter. But he'd been wrong.

She needed to know about all threats. There was no way to protect Everett otherwise.

She sank down on the couch, her head in her hands. Who was she kidding? She was here because she couldn't protect her son. She needed Talib, but his deception of silence was not acceptable and she would tell him that immediately. But it wasn't just him, there were things that she hadn't told. No more secrets, she promised herself.

She went over to the desk and grabbed a blank piece of paper and a pen, and began writing it all down, everything that had happened, from the beginning. For there was more to all of this than even she knew. She was sure of it. Something far darker and more deadly lurked and she was putting her trust in one man, believing that he would know what to do. She trusted that he would find the truth and would be fair. For in doing this, trusting him, she stood to lose her son to the power that was Al-Nassar. He could take Everett and there was nothing she could do about it. It broke her heart to think of it, but considering everything, it might be best for Everett and that was all that mattered.

No matter how much it would break her heart to let him go.

Chapter Twelve

Talib ran a hand through his hair.

In a suite beside Sara's, his work had only begun. He'd just ended a call from Barb Almay, who headed office research in both their home office and their Wyoming branch. She'd traced Sara's movements from the past several months. He wondered what resources the boyfriend had hired here and where he'd gotten the funds to do so. From everything Sara had told him, the man had no funds. He ran a hand through his hair, thinking about what he did know. A trace on Sara's accounts had made it clear that she'd been telling the truth. Her last withdrawal was enough to get a flight here. After that, she was living on fumes. She had no money to give to anyone. But it was clear the amounts she had told him had been the amounts withdrawn, at the time she'd said, the last over two months ago and then she'd run. It was exactly as she'd told him, the states she'd fled to, the mindless menial jobs, all of it. He felt rather low to be doing this, but he didn't have a choice. The stakes were too high. He would not jeopardize either his son's life or Sara's for her feelings. She might feel compromised or, more than likely, angry when she found out, but that was the risk he needed to take.

He ran through the facts. There were too few of them and nothing was making any sense. From everything he knew, Tad Rossi had never entered Morocco. Someone within Morocco had to be involved. Someone with expertise, as they'd been able to rig the explosion in the hotel and almost carry off the kidnapping of his son. He had to get to the heart of who was running this toxic little scheme.

His thoughts were interrupted by a banging on his door and a woman's voice.

Sara.

He strode to the door, opened it and looked down at her slight frame almost completely hidden by the blanket that was draped over her shoulders and around their son. She was struggling with the weight of the boy. He took the sleeping toddler from her arms.

"Why didn't you tell me?" she demanded.

"Tell you what?"

If anyone hadn't been told anything, if anyone had the right to be angry, it was him. He said nothing, just watched her as she pushed past him, leaving the door hanging open. He closed it and followed her, baffled at how the anger he had been feeling had suddenly shifted to her and, more intriguingly, seemed justified. He was in an emotional sandpit. Instinctively, he lay the boy down on a beige leather couch that sat on the reverse wall of the one in her suite.

"Someone tried to steal Everett, kidnap him?" Her

voice was high, almost on the edge of hysteria. "What else aren't you telling me?"

His mind went back to those moments in the hotel. It was something they needed to discuss, but he wanted to have a clearer idea as to how it all fit before they did.

"Who told you?"

"That's not important, not right now."

She had a point. He'd felt wrong and justified at the same time about keeping the information from her. "I wasn't sure what had been going on. Until I did, there was no point saying anything that might get you unnecessarily upset."

"Unnecessarily upset," she said slowly, drawing out each syllable. "And you think that it wasn't wise that I knew as soon as possible so I could be more aware—prepared."

"You're right," he admitted. It was a fact that he'd struggled with and was only justified because he felt he could keep them safe here. But maybe knowing the truth would help her accept the boundaries necessary to keep them safe. Her suite within this hotel was the boundary.

"Sit down," he said, pointing to a chair.

She ignored his instruction and sat down on the edge of the couch by their son.

And then he told her everything he'd seen in the lobby of the Desert Sands Hotel. When only twelve hours ago fate had thrown them together and meeting his son meant that he had to save him first.

He came over to her, kneeled down in front of her and took her hands, squeezing them. "Sara."

"Don't." She shook her head, pulling her hands free. "This isn't about us."

Us.

That had all been so long ago and in the end, so regretful.

There were times in their romance that he'd acted more playboy than responsible lover. He had never denied that, but a relationship hadn't been what he wanted, no matter his feelings for Sara. He'd toyed with her and for that he was sorry. But none of what he had done justified what she had done.

"I get a call regularly at three fifteen in the morning," she said, breaking into his thoughts. "It's always been Tad on the other end. But not this time. The voice was robotic, like something generated by a computer maybe, but the tone, the message—all of it was the same."

Talib shook his head. "What's the significance of three fifteen?"

"It was the time that Everett was born."

In the early hours of the morning she'd given birth to his son. Regret ran through him, not of the boy's existence, but of so many other things that he didn't want to acknowledge. He looked at her, her slight build, her peaches-and-cream complexion and the honesty and hope mixed with fear that shone from her eyes. And in that moment he hoped it hadn't been difficult. He didn't want to think of it much more than that, for any consideration to those facts brought a tsunami of emotion that was overwhelming.

"What does he say?"

"It's rather the same each time," she said.

"Tell me," he said shortly. He didn't know what she believed but what he knew was that they didn't have much time. It sounded to him like her ex-boyfriend had just lost control and tipped the scales in favor of an unknown entity who was here in Marrakech. At least that was his best guess. How it had all come together was unknown. The unknown needed to be removed. For, it was the unknown that got people killed and the unknown that was his job to clear up as quickly as possible.

"He called to remind me that I owe him and that I'll lose my son if I don't come through. But like I told you, what he wants now, I can't give him." She shook her head.

"Until now," he said.

She didn't look at him at first, and when she did her eyes were full of such anguish that it almost broke his resolve. Despite the betrayal he still felt, he had an overwhelming need to protect her and now it was loaded with a surprising emotion, one that he couldn't quite identify. He pulled her up, taking her into his arms, feeling her soft curves against him. He'd thought once that letting her go had been a mistake, now he knew that it had been more than that. But so much had happened, so many life-altering things that she had gone through without him. Regret was beginning to overshadow his anger. Neither emotion was relevant or productive to attaining the one goal he needed to focus on—keeping their son safe. He ran a comforting hand along her shoulder before releasing her and stepping away.

"There's a lot of hurt in the past for both of us."

She looked up at him with surprise.

He offered her a smile that held more regret than humor. "I know, that's not what the old Talib would say. But I'm three years older and hopefully three years wiser. I hurt you…"

"It was a long time ago."

"It doesn't matter how long ago it was, what happened was monumental and now we have him." He had her hands, squeezing them as if that would reestablish a connection or help either of them understand what had broken between them.

She pulled away from him and he realized his mistake immediately. He'd used the word *we*. In her mind Everett was her son, he knew that and it was a point that he'd never concede. He might have missed out on over two years, but now Everett was as much his son as hers and he planned to make up for lost time. But all that was something they would hash out later.

"We," he said firmly, despite his thoughts. "He's my son and it will be a while before I forgive you, if I ever can," he warned. "But going forward I'm an equal parent."

"Equal," she repeated and there was a smile that was almost relief.

He didn't understand it. He'd just told her that he was in her life whether she wanted him to be or not.

A strand of hair flipped across her face. He reached with one finger to push it back and she jerked away from him.

"Sara!" He took her shoulders, squeezing them. She cringed and took another step away.

He frowned, dropping his hands and feeling outrage and shock at the same time. She was acting like a woman who had experienced physical violence at the hands of a man. That wasn't the Sara he knew, either. "Did someone...did he lay a hand on you?"

She didn't say anything.

"Sara, tell me. Please."

"Once. We broke up after that. But I would have, even if it hadn't happened."

He didn't curse despite choice words that mixed with the rage and boiled hot and furious, wanting, needing an outlet. He was only thankful that the man was an ocean away from him, for at this moment he would have killed him.

"He threatened you," he said thickly. "He laid a hand on you. I'll kill..." He put a hand on her shoulder. "Not literally, but I'd make it painful for him to function properly for a good long time."

"Thank you for that," she said softly. "But no, Talib. Don't ever. It could ruin your life."

"I won't murder the son of a—"

"Donkey," she suggested with a wry smile.

"Thank you," he said with a grin that was only half-sincere. Unless opportunity arrives during the investigation, he thought, but it was a thought she didn't need to know about. "One thing is sure," he said through tight lips. "He'll never touch either of you again."

"Be careful," she said softly. "He'll get what he deserves, legally."

"How did you meet him?" Even now, after hearing his name, he had no desire to say it.

"Tad was from Morocco, like you," she said, not sensing his withdrawal. "I went to a travel show on Morocco."

"Why?"

"Why do you think?" she said softly, glancing over at Everett. "I wanted Everett to know his heritage."

"You wanted to keep the baby in touch with his roots?"

"Don't look so surprised. He was living in America but eventually he needed to know his heritage. I was looking for safe options."

"Safe?"

"Never mind, Talib. It seems a long time ago. Anyway, I met him there."

"So there's a good chance he has family, friends, at the least, an acquaintance here," he said thoughtfully. The scene played out in his mind. His son in the arms of the maid, her words. It wasn't something he wanted to discuss with Sara. She'd given him all she could. It was clear that she knew little of her former boyfriend's connections. All of it was stressing her, he could see it in the taut lips that had once been full and the new line in her once smooth brow.

She handed him a piece of paper. "I've written

down everything that's happened, anything of any significance that might help you end this."

He scanned her notes. Some of the information was new, none of it earth-shattering enough to provide any clear clues or motive. He looked up, met her eyes and was hit by truths that disturbed him.

She had few funds and everything she had was going into their son. That was clear in the weight she'd lost and the hollows under her eyes.

He would protect them with his life. The burden wouldn't be shared. It would become his. Only once before had they had a case that had threatened those he loved. It involved his sister, Tara, and had happened almost a year ago. But this wasn't the same, he didn't love Sara, but his son… His thoughts dropped off. He didn't know what he felt. He'd never felt so conflicted, so emotionally off-kilter.

She shook her head, her mind clearly going back over their discussion. "I can't believe that Tad would do this—hire someone to kidnap him, if he even found the funds. I just can't believe it."

"I don't think it was a kidnapping as you're thinking of it. Not that that makes this any better."

"I don't understand. They were in the process of—"

"Kidnapping." He shook his head. "No. Making a child disappear for a few hours. Making a point. I've seen it done before. The other option, that is if Tad hasn't left American soil, is that the incident isn't related. That it was a crime of opportunity, nothing else."

"Thank goodness you were there." Relief softened her features. "You saved him. Thank you. You've already done so much, you've been investigating…" Her voice trailed off and she bit her trembling lower lip.

"I have my research team on it. In the meantime, we can protect you better at the family compound."

"No!" She shook her head. "I won't go there," she said with a note of finality.

He'd heard that tone before and knew that she was prepared to stand her ground. In her position, he wasn't sure he wouldn't do the same. The family compound was ideal but he'd known it was a long shot for her to agree to go. The compound was also the heart of his family. While it wasn't true, he knew that she'd feel like she'd given up her last bit of autonomy. But that was Sara, fiercely independent. He'd offered the option and hoped but he'd prepared for her refusal by securing her suite here.

"Sara." He went to her, taking her face in his hands, looking into her troubled eyes. He only wanted to comfort her. Instead he bent down and tasted the softness of her lips. As he remembered the passion of their romance, he claimed her with all the emotion that ran conflicted through him.

Her hands were on his shoulders and she pushed him gently back, brought him to reality.

"I'm sorry, I…"

"It won't happen again," she said softly. "Promise me."

"No need," he said as he turned away from her.

Chapter Thirteen

"I'm going to meet with Emir," Talib said and the words broke the silence that had hung in the room for the last few minutes.

"Now?" She frowned.

"I know." He gave her an off-kilter smile. "It's almost four thirty in the morning but he starts his day at five, sometimes sooner."

They were both wide awake. And while he was sure sleep was at least another day away for him, he doubted if it would be any different for her. The only one getting any sleep was the boy and a thought struck him that maybe it would be nice to have her company. He would cut short his trip to see Emir and then take her around to the family compound, maybe sway her mind to relocate there. It was an argument he wasn't ready to drop.

"Come with me. You can bring the baby."

"You said I was safe here," she said. "I'm not leaving, Talib. Just tell me it's safe."

"You are," he assured her. No matter how much he'd rather she go to the compound, he couldn't lie. He'd prepared for such a situation and now that she'd made it clear by refusing once again, that it was a done deal, it was time to tell her. "In fact what I haven't told you is that I've hired a twenty-four-seven guard duty. There'll be someone patrolling this hallway at all times. So if I'm not here and you need anything, anything at all—even…" He looked over at the boy. "Cookies or biscuits, whatever…"

"Biscuits," she said with a small laugh.

"You know what I mean, Sara. You have round-the-clock protection. The man who has the day shifts will be Andre." He went over to a desk in the far corner of the room and picked up a sheet of paper. "Here," he said as he handed it to her. "It has their names and shifts and a picture so you can verify their identity."

"You're frightening me."

"No, Sara. It's nothing to be frightened of." He leaned down and gave her a chaste kiss on the cheek. Yet he wanted to turn her to face him and kiss her hot and wet on the lips. He took a step away and turned to grab his keys off a small stand. "It's a necessity until we catch your blackmailer."

"I don't need a babysitter," she interrupted with determination running like steel through her voice. "I just needed you to know. To be on board with this. To…"

"Protect him." He nodded. "I know. And you need money, too, I'll have some wired to your—"

"Talib, no. You make my head spin. This is too

much. The money I mean. Thank you, but I won't accept unless this is a loan."

"No loan," he said. "Get the information to my assistant and she'll facilitate the transfer. I insist on not only protecting you and my son, but supporting him, too." He looked at her and ran a finger gently along her cheek.

He met her questioning gaze.

"I wish I could say no, but…"

"It's all right," he said. "My assistant will contact you."

She shook her head.

"You can trust her. Give her Tad's contact information and she'll get the money to him," he continued.

Her eyes were bright with tears. "I'll pay you back."

"Sara…" He touched her shoulder. "Let me do this. And as far as the blackmailing piece of camel dung, trust me, he won't get everything he wants—not yet. Only enough to buy some time."

"I don't understand," she said with a frown. "If he doesn't get what he wants he'll…"

"Do nothing," Talib said. "There's nothing he or whoever he is partnered with can do. Trust me, Sara. Holding back money may make him careless."

"Buy time," she murmured.

"Exactly," he agreed.

Enough time for him to take him down and have him drown in his own blood, he thought. They were words he would never say to her, in front of his son or otherwise. "And, it goes without saying when this is over, I'll be supporting my son."

Silence hung between them. If he was reading her emotions right, he would say she was stunned or possibly just in a state of disbelief. He wasn't sure what he expected, but it didn't feel right to think that she might have, in some way, expected the worst from him.

"And maybe you can get a few hours' sleep before I get back. You're right, you're probably better off here than trailing along after me. Besides, that would wake the baby."

She looked at him oddly.

"His name's Everett."

"I know," he said thickly, but the name stuck in his throat.

He picked up his son. Somehow he was able to think of him in terms of a relationship, as an entity but not as a name, an individual who somehow made their situation all too glaringly real.

"I'll walk you both back to your room." He gazed down at the bundle in his arms. He looked at Sara and circled her shoulders with his arm, drawing her along with him to the door.

She smiled, a rather tired effort, as she reached to open the door.

"As far as your blackmailer…" He met her eyes as if delivering a silent promise. "Like I said, we'll deal with him. I promise you, Sara, this will work out. No one will hurt either you or the boy."

She nodded.

He realized that again he hadn't referred to the child by name. He thought of him as his, but the name, somehow, in an odd way, meant acknowledging his son's mother. Because Everett was a name that he knew Sara loved. She'd once mentioned that if she ever had a boy, she'd call him by that name. Saying the name felt like he was accepting what she had done and in doing so, forgiving her for not telling him. He wasn't ready for that.

"WHAT'S GOING ON?" Emir asked as Talib slouched down into one of the leather chairs that had been his father's and his grandfather's before that. The leather sank beneath his weight, yet not so much that it still wasn't providing support.

The office was a place that he considered the heart of the family compound. It was a place that reminded him of the strength and loyalty of his family and where Nassar Security had begun.

"You look terrible, Talib," Emir said. "Something on your mind besides the obvious? I'm betting it's not the breach of security and the explosion at Ian's hotel either."

Talib looked at his brother and for a moment wondered why he was here. There was nothing Emir could do or say that would change any of it. Not the part that haunted him, the boy—his son.

"You know, don't you?"

"Sara came here with your son." Emir nodded.

Talib's eyes met his older brother's. He ran a hand through his hair. "It was that obvious?"

"I guessed," Emir said. "Am I right?"

Emir smiled in that all-knowing older-brother way that, through the years, had been nothing short of infuriating. This time there was too much on his mind to even think about it.

"That the boy is mine." He nodded. "That's what she says."

"What do you say?" Emir asked, his dark eyes clashing with Talib's, challenging him.

"How'd you know?" Talib asked instead.

"A blind man could see that, T. He's like seeing you when you were a kid."

"I can't believe she's here. That she never told me, that…"

"What are you going to do about it?"

He lurched to his feet, as if sitting for another moment was just too difficult. "I'll take responsibility."

"A given," Emir said easily. "But that doesn't answer my question."

Talib paced the room before turning to face his brother. "She's in trouble."

"I assumed as much," Emir said as he leaned back in his chair and folded his arms, his dark eyes fixed on him. "You mentioned once that she didn't like to travel. And yet, here she is halfway around the world. You two are no longer a couple—so why is she here? I couldn't think of anything else other than the fact that it's your business to protect and she needs help. What else could it be?"

Despite his oldest brother's look, which could be

disconcerting at times, this time it didn't faze him. His brother was bang on as usual.

"She's in trouble alright, in more ways than one," he said, thinking of the boy who was innocently caught in the midst of it all. He went on to tell Emir what he'd learned from Sara.

"Tad demanded money at regular intervals. Sara met them all until she ran out of money. It looks like he's not alone and they've upped their demands in the time since then and when she arrived in Morocco. I plan to give them a quarter of what they're asking. If whoever is at the helm of this in Morocco is outraged enough they might slip up. I've already set up a transfer of funds to meet part of the demand," Talib added.

"We've used the strategy before," Emir said.

Talib nodded. "I'm hoping it may flush them out."

"I'll assign another agent to that case I mentioned earlier," Emir said. "You need to stay focused on this. Has our office found anything?"

Talib went through what he knew. "I'm going back to the Sahara Sunset this morning."

Emir nodded approvingly. "You couldn't get a more impenetrable security. A crown prince or two has been known to stay there."

"You're telling me it was a good choice," Talib said with a self-deprecating smile.

"I don't need to," Emir said. "Old habits…"

"Never die," Talib said, referring to Emir's need as an older brother to give advice to his siblings.

"Have you considered moving them?"

"To the compound," Talib said. "Yes, in fact I already suggested it. She won't go."

"Probably not an issue. From what you've said you've eliminated, or at least controlled the possibility of any danger at the moment."

"Exactly. They're safe where they are. It's secure."

"But you're considering this as a temporary measure. Depending how long it takes to contain the danger?"

"If anything changes, I'll move them immediately. But the security there is every bit as tight as at the compound. And I know the security team well."

"Agreed. Is there anything I can do?" Emir asked.

"I'll let you know," Talib said as he moved to leave. He hesitated at the door before turning around. "Thanks," he said. "Sara's ex is a small-time crook but he's got someone contracted here that has me worried. Mainly because he's an unknown entity. I'll feel better when I have an ID on him. But one thing is clear—he has more resources than her ex-boyfriend."

"So who is he? Any ideas?"

"The ex-boyfriend's name is Tad Rossi and he has Moroccan roots. I'm assuming it could be anyone he had connections with here. It might be a deeper dig to find them then I thought."

"Really? The boyfriend was Moroccan too?"

"Apparently she has a type."

"A type?" Emir frowned.

"You know dark-haired, exotic—or so I've been told," Talib said with a grin. "Or maybe it's just tall, dark and handsome." He shoved his hands in his pockets. "Seriously, she met him at a Moroccan travel presentation. It appeared to be coincidental, but I don't believe in coincidence."

"She was singled out."

"It's a possibility I considered," Talib replied. "Despite that theory, he seems like a rank amateur. It won't take much to bring him down and close this case. Then I'll be available."

"Will you?"

"What do you mean?"

"Aren't you forgetting something?" Emir asked softly.

Talib met Emir's gaze and somehow he couldn't acknowledge the obvious reference his brother was making. It was all too big and too incomprehensible.

"You have a son, T," Emir said gravely. "Our family has an heir. Getting to know him might take a bit of your time."

An heir to the Al-Nassar wealth and history—it was inconceivable and he'd been treating it all so lightly. He frowned. When this was over, and only then, he needed to rethink his position, because he knew, as Emir had implied, that his son needed to be here—with him.

That wouldn't go over with Sara, but he'd have time to bring her around.

In the end, he knew she'd do anything to protect their son.

And he'd do anything to protect his family—even if it meant his own life.

Chapter Fourteen

"What do you have?" Talib asked as he answered a call from his youngest brother, Faisal. He wasn't surprised to hear from Faisal, considering that the trouble had originated in America. Faisal headed the Wyoming office of Nassar Security. As a result, he was their go-to person for most things relating to the United States. They'd worked through the night on this one, no different than any other case.

"Barb Almay contacted me," Faisal said, referring to their head researcher. "She was doing some research for you and hit a sticking point. Tad Rossi was placed under arrest, but she couldn't get any more information than that. So she called me."

"Under arrest." Talib frowned. "And?"

"I pulled some strings here and discovered that the man you're looking for is now out of the picture."

"What do you mean?"

"Tad Rossi was arrested yesterday for assault of an elderly woman at a banking machine near the state border of New Hampshire and Maine. The woman fought back and with the help of a passerby, he was restrained and held until police arrived."

"Good Samaritan?"

"Exactly. You'll be interested in this—he had a newly issued passport on him as well as a small bag."

"Needed money for the flight over?"

"My guess," Faisal said.

"So now he's, at least for the time being, in a jail cell."

"Not exactly. He was killed early this morning. Attacked by another prisoner while being transferred from the police holding cells."

"You're joking," Talib said, but it wasn't a question. Faisal would never joke about something like that. "Do you have anything else on him?"

"Not a lot. He's been in the States for the last twelve years. Any ties he has in Morocco reveal nothing from this end. You might have a better chance of uncovering something where you are."

"Thanks, bro," Talib said as he disconnected. He flipped the phone in his hand as he pondered the situation. Before this news he'd hoped to interrogate Sara's ex-boyfriend and find out who he'd contracted here. Now, they'd lost that connection. Whoever was here was working alone and the danger had escalated drastically, for the threat was now not only anonymous, but also connected to no known entity. It was reduced, as Sara had described, to a robotic voice on a phone line.

THE DARKNESS WAS just beginning to thin as Talib pulled into the parking lot of the Desert Sands Hotel.

Shadows shifted across the lot, where only four other vehicles were parked. He knew one was Ian's—the others, he could only assume belonged to upper management, security, or other, similar such people. He didn't envy his friend being dealt such a massive hand of trouble, but Ian would persevere and succeed. He always did.

He got out, giving the car door a light push as it closed with a slick precision that didn't make a sound.

He glanced around.

He was alone. Everything was deadly silent.

There was no parking lot attendant. He frowned. There should have been at least a contracted guard considering everything that had happened.

A breeze ran through the lot. The shadows seemed to shift and then everything was still. He looked around. There was nothing. He was jumpy. Like this was his first case, his first assignment. It was a poor analogy for he'd never been jumpy before, even then, in his youth—in the beginning of his career. He wasn't sure why he was jumpy now.

He stopped, caught in his own musings.

He had a son.

It was incomprehensible.

The kid would be the first of the next generation in his family. And he'd missed over two years of his life. Something shifted. The shadows seemed to move around him. And, on the horizon, a streak of sunlight cut through the dawn sky, tantalizing, in a way teasing with the fact that soon it would take back the night. But his mind was occupied with other things and he didn't hear footsteps until he was swinging around, swinging into danger.

He was aware of it immediately, and too late. He should have dumped the thoughts and pulled his gun. That was his first mistake. To say he was overwhelmed was an understatement. But that was no excuse. His mind told him to reach for his gun, his fingers moved as if in that direction. He would have done it, given another second.

He only had enough time to duck as he tried to make out the blur, the shadow of a man coming at him. It was not only too late, but also not enough. The only thing the move did was make sure that the bat his attacker was wielding caught him on the edge of his shoulder instead of the side of his head. He was thrown off balance and had to fight to keep on his feet. The pain that ran through his shoulder was sharp and immobilizing. He could see the bat coming down again. This time he had an arm up as he grabbed the man's wrist, but it was again too late to stop the bat and he was only able to slow its progress. The bat connected with his upper arm and pain rocketed through him. He twisted the man's wrist with everything he had, ignoring his own pain, pushing to hear a snap of bone.

But the snap didn't come and he was in too awkward a position. He let go, unable to hold on any longer. He lost his balance, but caught his fall with one hand—his right, the injured arm. The pain ran up his arm into his throbbing shoulder.

He looked up as he struggled to stand.

Dark hair, wiry, a half head shorter than him but thick and wearing a soft, camel-colored jacket. They were all facts that his brain registered in the muted light that hung somewhere between day and night.

He was sure his attacker didn't have a gun. He would have shot him by now if he had. That spoke volumes. A small-time crook, a street hood. Quick money. He was being taken out by what appeared to be a rank amateur. But there was little time for pride. Instead, the thoughts were quick and automatic as he struggled to pull his gun.

Again he was too late. The man got a second wind and rushed him. Talib's hands weren't as skilled or as quick as usual. His dominant right hand was bruised, temporarily crippled from the earlier blow. Otherwise, he would have taken him down at the outset. Instead, he grabbed his attacker's arm with his left hand, making him drop the bat, grimaced at his own pain and plowed through it. The bat fell to the pavement and rolled out of reach.

One of the blows had hit the side of his head and he was seeing stars. He had to get it together. He pulled himself upright with a willpower that had seen him through a stint with the Royal Moroccan Army.

This was inconceivable and unthinkable, but the truth was that he'd had his guard down. He deserved all of this and more for his own stupidity. But he needed to get out of this.

But even realizing that, something else occurred to him—he had to fight harder or he was going down.

He had let it go too far. The advantage of surprise had been everything for his attacker.

Sara depended on him. The truth of that had him pushing to stand upright.

He managed to get in a few blows of his own and his attacker was struggling. If he could just get control of himself, he knew that he could come out the victor. He didn't keep himself in peak condition to lose to a street hood. The hours he'd spent in the gym wouldn't be wasted. His head spun but he forced himself to stand up.

He had an advantage. He was armed, his fuzzy brain reminded him. His attacker wasn't. The bat still lay a distance away on the pavement. He reached for his gun. That's when he found himself grabbing air.

This was outrageous.

Then he had his gun in his hand and then somehow he didn't. It was on the pavement and he wasn't sure how that had happened, but his hand was stinging like it had been hit. He had no weapon. This was a fight using hand-to-hand combat.

He looked up. He couldn't have been more wrong. The gun and the bat were still out of reach on the pavement, but his attacker was no longer unarmed. The morning sun was clearing the darkness away, sending streaks of light across the pavement and reflecting off the knife in his hand that glinted for a split second, almost blinding him.

A switchblade.

The realization seemed to change everything. It was like the last push in his army survival training, only it was more immediate than that. This was life or death like he'd never faced before.

Suddenly his head cleared, and the stars were gone. He had one chance here, one chance to live or die. There was no more time for anything but the skills he had and the gut instinct to move in the right direction at the right time. To be offensive or defensive, to make the best choice of either of those options. His weapon was his bare hands and the power of his mind.

The man was rushing him.

He twisted left, away from his attacker, who was swift and lethal despite his smaller size. He was wearing a hoodie and dressed in black, his face indistinguishable from so many others on the street. Talib bent low and came up with the edge of his hand on the man's already injured wrist.

The man grunted—he'd scored a hit but the switchblade was still tight in his hand and coming at him again. The morning sun was streaking across the pavement, reflecting off the knife in his hand and off his face. There was a hard look in his eyes and an unfocused look in one of them. The glint lasted a second, shifted and almost blinded him.

The man glared at him, the eye connection was brief, a millisecond, no more. But in that look a challenge was laid out. He could see the pain behind the challenge. He'd injured him badly. Still, he held the knife. Now, the switchblade came down again, close, slicing his shirt just below his rib cage as his hand caught the man's wrist, sending the knife short of its target. The man snarled as he pushed him off balance. That was all the time that Talib needed to gain the advantage.

This time, as the man came in for another attack, he was ready for him. He came in from the side as the knife sliced through air. He had his attacker's wrist. He twisted and felt a bone crack as the man grunted in pain. The switchblade dropped and Talib's foot came down on it. At the same time, a knee hit his groin slightly off center, but still sending him reeling. His palm touched the pavement and he saw that his gun was just to his left. He reached and had it.

But his attacker had had enough.

He was already running across the parking lot, holding one arm against his chest. The man was too far away for Talib to have an accurate shot.

"We'll take your son!" the attacker shouted hoarsely, before he disappeared past the fringes of the lot and into what remained of the night.

The words seemed to echo over and over through the parking lot, or maybe it was through his shell-shocked brain. A son and a threat all at the same time. He ached where no man should ever have to ache. He was immobilized. He lost track of the minutes before he was on his feet and ready to walk.

He was alone. His entire body was bruised and he knew that he would feel the effects for a while. He hadn't been bruised up this bad in a long time.

He looked around, getting his bearings, making sure that he wasn't going to be assaulted again in a surprise attack. Nothing moved.

He stood there for a moment just taking breaths, combing the shadows as if somewhere on the edges of the pavement his attacker still lurked.

Chapter Fifteen

"What the hell happened to you, man?" Ian asked as Talib came in through the service entrance.

Talib tried not to favor his left leg, where his attacker had kicked him, or his shoulder that had also been clipped. They were what pained him most; he wouldn't think of what else hurt.

"You need to see a doctor."

"I'm fine. Looks worse than it is."

"You're sure?"

Ian's look of concern almost made him laugh.

"Definitely. Besides, there's no time," Talib said impatiently. "Was the surveillance camera on the guest parking lot working this morning?"

"Of course," Ian replied. "That was one of the first security measures I put into place. Exactly as you recommended."

"I need to see it."

Ian frowned. "You're not saying…" His dark brows drew together. "This is more than a security issue." His gaze roved over him. "Someone messed you up good, my friend."

"There was no one in the parking lot, Ian. No security."

He looked at Talib as if he'd forgotten the initial state his friend had been in, as if the shock of first sight had only now been addressed. "What happened?"

"I was attacked in the parking lot. Guy with a bat and a switchblade."

"Sweet mother," Ian muttered. "That's why you asked about the camera. I can't believe this. You were right all along that I should have steered clear of this hotel. Purchasing it might have been premature."

"No. You might have led too soon off the block with opening but otherwise…" Talib shook his head. Bad move, his head was aching…deeply. "Do you have an aspirin?"

"Yeah, sure—give me a minute." Ian disappeared and returned a few minutes later with a bottle of pills and a glass of water.

Talib swallowed a couple of the painkillers and drained the glass before putting it down and turning to look at his friend.

"Crap, you look bad," Ian muttered.

"I've been worse," Talib said. There had been the time when he'd crashed a Ferrari and ended up three days in a hospital and with a scar that ran the length of his right thigh. That had been worse. This time he was still walking, although the pounding in his head was difficult to ignore. There was no point dwelling on it. His body would heal in its own time. Unfortunately, he didn't have that time to waste. He needed to keep moving and protect Sara and his son. "Let's run the footage and see if we can pin an ID on this piece of camel dung. He had his first and last run at me or anyone I care about," he said, thinking of Sara and the boy.

Fifteen minutes and a few calls later, they had a lead, and the name of a Moroccan national. He was a man with a long list of petty crimes and with no obvious link to either Sara or his son.

"Interesting," Talib said. His headache had calmed to a dull roar. He looked at the name he'd scrawled on a piece of paper along with a few other bits of information they'd dredged up. It was a name that meant nothing to anyone. Hired by someone to take him out or, at the least, ward him off.

The question was, who had hired him?

It HADN'T BEEN EASY, but Habib finally got the information he needed. He knew where she was, where the kid was. For a while it had seemed like the whole scheme had fallen apart, but now it was moving forward.

He gritted his teeth. To think he had started life as one of them. Rich like all the rest. He'd attended the same privileged primary school and then, because of his father's foolhardiness, they had lost it all. He remembered the school-yard taunts. Kids could be cruel, but what he remembered the most was the fact that Talib's father, Ruhul Al-Nassar, could have saved his family from the financial and social ruin that followed. Ruhul could have been a silent partner in the financial opportunity that his father had presented to him. If Al-Nassar had invested in the oil company his father had had a chance to partner in, they would have been rich once again. But Al-Nassar had refused. He'd said the investment wasn't something he was interested in. In fact, he'd hinted that his father wasn't capable of turning the business into a lucrative enterprise. He'd even pointed out his past failures. Listening silently on the other side of a closed door, he'd heard it all. His father didn't have the money to do it alone and the opportunity had slipped out of his hands almost as quickly as the life of luxury they had known disappeared. Instead, the mighty Al-Nassar had offered his father a job and, worse than that, his father had taken it.

He'd hated the Al-Nassars from that moment on. He could have gotten over the school-yard taunts for those few remaining months at private school. He could have skated over the public school education for his last six years. But he'd never forget the chance that was lost to his family because of an Al-Nassar. His father was dead now and so was Ruhul Al-Nassar. The grudge had been carried to the next generation, to Talib, the man who, as a boy, had once been his classmate. He'd always secretly blamed Talib. He was sure that somehow, in some way, he had influenced his father's decision. He'd never know but he'd go to his grave believing that. He hated them all but he hated Talib most of all. Now, he finally had a chance to get it all back.

He considered his options. The idiot Tad had been

wrong. Kidnapping the child was exactly what he needed to do. Just short-term. He didn't need the kid longer than that. Al-Nassar had to know by now that the kid was his and he'd do anything, give anything, to get him back. He knew about family loyalty and he knew all about them. They fought for what was theirs. It was a trait that he would use to his advantage.

He lit a cigarette and took a drag. The thought of what all of this could do to those who had made him feel so inferior ran through his body, in a shiver that snaked down his spine.

Tad had told him they only needed a fright and he'd initially agreed to that.

But he was having doubts now. They already knew the kid was the key to everything. This time he would be successful. If they thought money would save the kid, then the Al-Nassars would throw money at him. It was a brilliant plan and surprisingly simple. Once he had the money it was game over and the desert was pretty unforgiving. If the kid was hardy, maybe he'd come through in one piece. He didn't really care how that turned out. He'd handle the kid next time and it would be serious, a real kidnapping. Meanwhile, Al-Nassar had moved her and the kid, and it had taken him until now to find out where. By this time tomorrow he'd have the kid and be long gone and Al-Nassar would quit playing games with him and give him every dime he demanded.

In fact, with Al-Nassar in the game, it was going to be a challenge, but that just upped the fun. The Sahara Sunset was one of the best as far as security. But no security was impenetrable. He'd gotten most of the information he needed—now all that was required was time and an opportunity. In a career of crime that he'd honed over the last decade, he'd learned that there was always a weak link. There was always someone who could be bought and whose skills could be used. It had taken him less time to find the hotel than it had to find that link that could be bought. Only an hour ago, the necessary money had changed hands. Now, he just needed to set the plan in motion.

Chapter Sixteen

"The police caught and lost your attacker," Ian said in that quick way that was unique to him. He tended to get straight to business and avoided any pleasantries or time wasters, as he liked to call them. It was what worked for both of them. "I just spoke to the detective on the case."

"What do you mean lost?" Talib asked.

"The bugger slipped police restraints as he was being transferred. Had him on a minor traffic violation and it was only your mention of the lazy eye that had our officer frisk him and find the switchblade." He gave Talib the name of the suspect, but it meant nothing to him.

Talib returned to the Sahara Sunset later that day with a feeling of relief and of coming home.

He knocked on the door, not wanting to scare her.

"It's me, Talib," he added for good measure.

The door opened and her smile of relief almost melted his heart. "Talib," she said. "Where have you been?" And that was followed by an immediate gasp. "What happened to you?" Her hands were on his cheeks, as she gently ran her fingers down his bruises. "Who did this?" she asked in a tone like she was about to launch war on the perpetrator. She had his hand before he could answer any of that and dragged him over to the couch. In truth, he followed willingly, rather enjoying the attention.

"You need ointment, bandages…" She tsked.

"I'm fine, Sara, really." He patted the seat beside him. "Sit down with me. That's all I need right now is you."

"I can't believe it. What happened?" she asked as she sat down close beside him. Her bare arm rubbed against his and the thought of his bruises went to the back of his mind.

It was like being met by a wife's loving scolding. He'd never thought that of a woman, never thought he'd want to be in that position. The words were oddly unromantic and yet they made him feel as though his world just turned around.

"Talib," she said, shifting on the seat so that she was turned sideways to look at him. "I was worried."

"I would have been here sooner. I had a bit of a scuffle."

She brushed his arm with her hand. "I'm so sorry, Talib. I should never have come. I've put you in danger, disrupted your life. I'm sorry."

"The only mistake you made, Sara," he said thickly, "was not finding me sooner."

Thirty minutes later, as they sat together over coffee, there was rustling in the bedroom and the sound of their son's voice chattering in his version of English and baby talk. The mix was uniquely his own.

Sara stood up. He touched her arm with gentle fingers. "Please," he said. "Let me. I've never gotten him up from a nap."

Something in her face broke, like she might cry. He leaned down and kissed her. "I didn't mean that as a jibe. I really meant that I want to make up for lost time," he said.

"I know," she said softly.

Later, they ordered supper, a pizza, and enjoyed it together as a family. They were moments they would all remember. He stayed with her through that night, spooning her, feeling her soft curves and realizing that restraint was more difficult than he thought.

But he knew that he had to get moving. He didn't have the luxury of hanging around a hotel suite. It was his job to keep them safe.

His phone rang early the next morning and he answered to hear Barb's voice. "The suspect was last seen leaving one of the seedier areas of the Medina the evening before the attack." She gave him the address that they both knew housed more criminals than upstanding citizens.

"Possibly where he lives," Talib mused. "Or there was some sort of business dealings, or a myriad of things." He considered the options. "Not a great area," he said. "Anything else?"

"Still working on it. This is a tough one. There isn't much information easily available."

"None of your research is easy, Barb," Talib said with a laugh. "You're the best. Keep digging."

"Always."

He disconnected. There was only so much that could be found by their desk-bound researchers. He needed to get back in the field and check the address out.

"I've got to go," he said to Sara who'd been awakened by the call. It was just after 6:00 a.m. "Are you going to be all right?" he asked.

"I'm fine, Talib. We'll be fine," she reiterated. "Everything is secure. You do what needs to be done to make sure our son is safe." She hesitated, then took his right hand in both of hers. "Be careful. Don't do anything risky," she said. "Promise me."

He couldn't do that. Instead he leaned down and kissed her, wanting to pull her into his arms and offer more comfort than that brief kiss. Instead he left her with the promise that he'd see her soon.

Thirty minutes later Talib stood outside a rundown apartment building on the edge of one of Marrakech's oldest souks. Unlike the other areas, this particular section didn't have the vibrancy that drew the tourists and locals alike. Much of what might once have been heritage buildings were now weathered and broken. He passed a small, gray, rectangular building, which was wedged between two bigger buildings of a similar style, before arriving at his destination—a decrepit, four-story brick structure.

Farther down an alleyway, two white-haired men were smoking and talking. Both of them were too far away to ID him and neither of them paid any attention to him. He could slip in and out. A check with the super had confirmed that the tenant worked an early morning shift leaving well before six in the morning and returning to the apartment later in the afternoon. Hopefully, there was evidence in the apartment of who he was, who he knew and, better yet, who he might be associated with.

He jimmied the lock on the main door and slipped inside. He was met by a rush of stale, hot air that made him want to breathe as little as possible. The smell of something rancid, like cooking oil, wafted through the air—it was an unwelcome stench. There was no one else around. He took the concrete stairs, one at a time, with caution. The staircase was steep and narrow. The apartment was at the end on the second floor and as he stood outside of it, silence seemed to tick around him.

He put his ear to the wooden door. No sound. A door banged shut on the floor above him and his hand jerked back from the knob. He looked around. There was no one, nothing near him. Minutes later he was inside. The room was meager. Directly in front of him was a cot and to his right, a small television. There was a bathroom to his left, the only other room unless you counted a closet and an open-area kitchenette. He stepped farther in, moving around a stack of travel magazines.

"Going somewhere?" he murmured. The possibility was there—if this was their man, that he was picking the next destination where he could take the money and run. But there were no answers from a stack of magazines.

He stepped deeper into the room. Despite the fact that clothes and paper were strewn across the bed, they were arranged in an oddly organized way. It was a contradiction and yet it was clearly a pattern. He lifted a magazine from the bed.

A piece of pale yellow note paper slipped out from the pages of the magazine. There was a name on that paper. It was a name that wasn't unfamiliar to him. It didn't necessarily mean anything, but he'd gone to primary school with a boy by that name. It wasn't a common name. And there was a phone number. He grimaced at the thought of calling the number out of the blue, and saying what? What did Habib Kattanni have to do with a two-bit criminal who had fled detection? He frowned. His mind went back to the fact that Habib had gone to school with him. It was years ago and he couldn't imagine what the connection might be now. In fact, logically he'd like to say there was no connection, but the evidence seemed to be hinting otherwise. That gave rise to the question that the man might have the same name as the boy he'd gone to school with, but there the similarity stopped. Same name—different person. They were all things that needed to be followed up on. He thought back, remembering the boy who had been there for a term, maybe two—he wasn't sure. And then he'd left. There'd never been any explanation. What he remembered was his father saying something about the disgrace of it all. His father would have known for he'd employed Habib's father for a brief time after what everyone referred to as the scandal. Unfortunately, his father was no longer around for answers.

Talib looked at the paper and tried to dredge up any memory of the man. But there was nothing. It had been a long time ago.

Habib.

The few memories he had weren't good. He remembered that he was a whiney, unlikeable kid, but that didn't mean anything. Kids were a lot of things before they matured and became who it was they were meant to become. He couldn't see anyone he had gone to school with sinking to this. But why was Habib's name here, in this apartment? Was it a case of same name, different identity?

He stuffed the paper in his pocket and did a thorough check of the room. Whoever he was, he'd left in a hurry, but he'd taken almost everything of importance with him. None of it was matching what the super had said. The evidence he saw was looking like the tenant wasn't coming back. Ten minutes later, he was finished. He'd found nothing except the one name that led him into the shadows of his past—to when he was a boy.

He paused in the doorway as he contemplated the abject poverty so in opposition to the homes that anyone who had gone to his primary school had come from. Had the unsub contracted this man to attack him? And how was Habib linked into all of this, or was he? Had Habib hired someone to attack him? That made no sense, but if he hadn't, who had? What motivation did he have? The connection, the link, was the dead boyfriend, Tad. But dead men didn't talk.

He left, closing the door behind him, making sure to leave no evidence that he'd been there. Despite his belief that his parking-lot assailant was gone, he made sure that no one saw him as he left. But there was no one around, the cramped, age-greased corridor was as silent as when he'd arrived.

Outside, the narrow street was crowded with people and the occasional donkey. A slight man on a Vespa wound his way slowly through the throng.

Talib slipped into the crowd. His clothes were as worn as anyone else's in the area. He'd made sure to haul out the clothes he used to do some of the mechanic work on his vehicles. This wasn't an area where designer clothes and pressed shirts would fit. He wasn't much of an actor and he knew that how he presented himself was different than the working class that held the majority in the area. If someone questioned his appearance... But it didn't matter much anyway—the man he was after had already run.

He passed another alley, and saw a man of average height and build, and in faded jeans and an olive-green T-shirt watching him from the shadows.

Then the man motioned to him.

What the hell? Talib thought as he watched the man jerk his head to the alley, as if indicating he should follow.

The man disappeared again into the shadows.

He moved into the head of the alley. There was no one around him. He had his gun in one hand and yet it seemed like overkill. But he wasn't taking any chances. The man seemed to have disappeared. He could go forward or back out—this could be a trap. Just as he decided to back up and return to the busy shopping area behind him, he felt the presence of someone. He had no time to turn or duck.

The blow came before he could react. It was silent and even more lethal because of it. As Talib fell he could only think of one name—Sara. He had to get up. He had to go to her. Instead he kept falling, down, down as if the spiral was out of control and would never end. It finally did end as consciousness left him.

Chapter Seventeen

Sara looked at her watch and gritted her teeth—her stomach clenched and she felt sick. She hadn't heard from Talib since early this morning. She'd counted on him and somehow, in some way, he was letting her down.

She kept thinking the worst and it was making her crazy. That and the fact that she was trapped, imprisoned by a promise she'd made to Talib to stay in her suite. There was nowhere to go and no one to talk to. It was maddening.

Talib hadn't called as he had promised and he'd been gone for over seven hours.

"Where are you?" she murmured. Her worry and boredom were building in conflicting degrees.

She told herself that she shouldn't be worried, Talib knew what he was doing. She shouldn't be bored, either. She wasn't being held in a barren cell. She had every amenity. And if it wasn't available, whatever she might need was only a phone call away. There was a bodyguard, security Talib had called him, who, although not at the door at all times, was usually in the vicinity. One of the men that Talib had assigned, Andre, was the only one she'd seen so far. Andre knocked on her door at regular intervals to ensure that they were fine and that they weren't needing anything. He didn't lurk in the hallway, but she knew that he was always somewhere close by. He was amiable enough and she'd even teased him about a girl when he'd taken a call that was clearly not business. He had an easy smile, dark cropped hair, intense dark eyes and a physique that would deter most villains. He looked exactly like what he was—muscle for hire—unless you got to know him as she had. She'd learned that there was a soft spot with Andre and it was children. It was only with Everett that he turned completely to mush. His smile softened as he spoke baby talk to the boy and made him smile with his exaggerated facial expressions. Some were so absurd that Sara even found herself smiling.

But the visits from Andre were brief and the confinement was driving her crazy. She took a breath and then another as if to calm herself, or at least to redirect her thoughts. But there was no getting around it, the suite was claustrophobic despite what initially had seemed its expansive size. They'd been here too long. While there was no lack of things to watch on television or games that had been delivered to her room, everything had been toddler-centric. Despite Talib's company last night, she was alone now and feeling it. She was about to go out of her mind.

If nothing else, they needed to get out of this room. They were both restless and with Everett that meant his mood was going south fast. In the last five minutes he'd gone from whimpering to tears and she knew that a screaming fit wasn't too far away. The terrible twos had hit and sometimes there was just no calming him.

Soon, she was desperate to stop his screams and tears. He hadn't had one of these fits in weeks and really, she'd experienced this kind of meltdown only a few times in the past. What she knew was that without diversion, this was poised to become epic. Everett was stubborn, as toddlers can be, and was testing the edges of his world and his own sense of autonomy. She knew she'd been lucky so far. Thanks to the long trip, the strange environment and her own stress, she knew Everett was on edge. She was surprised that this hadn't come sooner.

Everett shrieked louder and higher, and then gulped, more than likely gaining energy for his next howl, and within a minute she was right. She needed a solution fast. This hotel might be luxurious and well-built, but insulation only blocked so much noise. In a regular hotel, someone would already be pounding on the walls for them to be quiet. She was betting it was only a matter of time here.

They needed a break from this suite. The hotel was safe, Talib had said so himself. She wouldn't do anything foolish, like step outside or stray from any areas that weren't well trafficked and secure. Her thoughts broke off as she smiled at that. Talib had told her that the hotel had security cameras on every floor, and in every area. Add to that a security team, one of whom she was on a first-name basis with, and there was no reason to worry. Besides, she wasn't planning to be gone long—ten, maybe fifteen, minutes. Just enough to calm Everett and regain her sanity.

There was no one that she needed to tell where she was going or what she was doing. Andre was on a late lunch break and it would be another thirty minutes before he returned. He'd knocked on the door only fifteen minutes ago to see if there was anything she needed. She'd assured him everything was fine, but it was the calm before the storm.

"When did you speak to Talib last?" Emir asked one of their office staff, and her answer had him concerned.

"The police had an identification on the man who attacked him at the Desert Sands parking lot. From that I found an address. Barb gave the information to Talib just after six this morning and we haven't heard anything from him since. I left a text for him to call four hours ago, but I haven't heard anything." The dark-haired, petite woman was their latest hire. Rania had turned out to be quick and efficient, digging up information in record time.

Emir shook his head. He didn't like the passage of time. That was a problem. He expected their agents, brothers or not, to check in when flying solo on a case. Especially one where he really should have been assigned backup. It was only Talib's request and the nature of the case that had him holding back from assigning another agent.

His brother had been out of communication for over seven hours. Again, considering the nature of the case and the fact that it was contained within the city limits of Marrakech, a lapse in communication was troubling. As a result, his senses were on alert. If everything was going right, then this didn't happen in their business, not on a case like this. They were all too well-trained, too conscientious. There was only one reason for this and it didn't bode well—something had happened.

Rania gave him the address that Barb had earlier given to Talib. He was pulling on a bulletproof vest as he headed out the door. He reached for his gun to make sure it was tucked in place under his waistband, ready at a moment's notice.

Chapter Eighteen

When Talib woke, the banging in his skull made him want to close his eyes again. He didn't have that luxury. He needed to stay awake, stay focused and figure out where he was and what kind of dung pile he'd landed in.

The pain was blinding.

He gave in and briefly closed his eyes, but only in an effort to get control of the pain. When he opened them again, he could see nothing but darkness, or at least that's what he initially thought. His eyes were barely open, not enough to get a good visual on anything—light, dark, nothing. He took conscious breaths, closed his eyes and opened them again. Wherever he was, he was in a place that smelled of dirt. Graveyard dirt. Bad image, he thought. Must, he was smelling must and lying on something hard. There was a flicker of light overhead. Where was he? How long had he been out and was he alone? They were questions that all needed to be answered before he made a move.

He remembered bits of what had happened. The

man, smaller than he, had come from nowhere. He hadn't had a chance to get a good look at him. He could have been the same man from the parking lot attack, or someone totally different. Because before he could turn and confront him, he'd been hit on the back of the head. It was only his earlier injuries that had slowed him down and allowed this to happen. After that there had been nothing, until now. He wasn't sure how much time had passed or where he was.

He should have asked for backup. That was his oversight.

He reached up with his bound hands to where the thin line of light sifted into his prison. A board was what was over his head. He could feel the wood. From what he could piece together, it was the floor just above him, some sort of trapdoor over a shallow storage area. Had they decided that taking out the father was better than the son? His mind whirred with possibilities. Were they just taking him out, out of the way so that they could take his son next? He bit back pain and panic. He needed to get control of both his emotions and the pain.

He lay still, trying to get his bearings, trying to figure out his next move and how he was going to get out of here. He was used to thinking on his feet, but not with his head thumping the way it was. He took a breath and then another. He'd learned a long time ago that in a crisis one should get a plan together. He couldn't burst out of his prison not knowing what lay on the other side. A thin shard of light grazed across his arm, bouncing off of broken tile just to the left of him. It was like someone had begun a cellar and then stopped and what remained was a shallow hole beneath the floor. It made no sense unless one had planned this in advance. Or was this a temporary prison? But that made no sense, either.

He stilled his thoughts, listening. There was no sound. There hadn't been any sound in the minutes he'd been conscious. He was fairly certain that wherever he was, he was alone.

He let his thoughts shift from his current predicament to his greatest worry.

Sara. He had to get to her, to warn her. More importantly he needed to protect her, for this was much more deadly, much more immediate, than he had thought. She was all that stood between their son and danger. He knew that she'd defend him with her life. He couldn't allow things to get to that point.

His thoughts were clearer now. They knew who he was. That was the only explanation. It had taken two attacks but their intent was to take him out. It was his own fault that they were close to succeeding. He'd let emotion fog the case and in doing that he'd underestimated the opponent. He needed to get back in the field to protect what he cherished most—his family.

"Let's go for a walk," Sara said to Everett, who was sniffling and red-faced. She spoke to him as if he was an adult. She often did that, speaking as if he understood the idea that walks often calmed him down. Her thought was to go to the hotel gift shop, maybe even a snack shop. Whatever stores were available here, she didn't know, as she'd had no time to explore. She was like a prisoner within the opulence of her suite. Somehow she'd never thought her visit would turn out like this. For that was all it was, a visit. She hadn't thought beyond that. It had been a flight of desperation, a cry for help that was turning out far different than she could ever have imagined. But she hadn't changed plans, this trip had an end date—return tickets booked and no resolution to her problem in sight. She pushed that thought from her mind.

"We'll go to the store," she said. In all probability they would be stores selling high-end products and designer goods. Even that would be helpful. Oddly, Everett always liked shopping. He was distracted by all the different things he saw on the shelves. It often made it a challenge for her, but it was exactly what she needed now. She imagined that the shelves might be filled with expensive trinkets. Shiny things that would only cause her grief as he reached for them, but would, more importantly, provide a distraction for him.

"Cracker," he demanded, waving his chubby hand. He hiccupped before bursting into a fresh bout of wails.

The fridge had been restocked, but crackers hadn't been included. She could phone and they'd be brought up immediately, but that wasn't the point.

She smiled at Everett and he snuffled and rubbed his eyes with the back of his fists. He was in a lull. Right now, his mood could go either way.

Five minutes later they reached the main floor without incident. There, the lobby was a pleasant surprise. The staff was courteous and willing to help, and directed her to a small snack shop that carried the animal crackers Everett loved. She also found a few shops that were entertaining enough for a small boy. She let Everett walk. She held his hand but her attention was fixed on everything around her. She watched for danger, trusted no one and paid attention to her environment. Someone had tried to kidnap Everett once and she wouldn't let it happen again.

Twenty minutes later they were heading back to their room. It was a different elevator ride than their earlier one, where Everett had hiccupped and sobbed the entire descent to the main floor. Now, he was smiling and she had managed to relax somewhat although she would never—could never—tone down her vigilance.

She stepped out of the elevator and turned to her right, heading for their suite. She passed one door, the carpet no less soft and luxurious beneath her feet than it had been the first time.

Twelve feet from her room, she stopped.

"No," she murmured.

"No," Everett repeated with a smile.

"Shh," she said as she put a finger to her lips and juggled him in one arm.

He nodded his head and smiled. He was slipping from her grip. She boosted him higher and his smile broadened. He put a finger to her lips.

She left his finger there, barely noticing. Instead

her gaze was caught by what she saw in front of her. She took a step backward.

The door to her hotel suite was open.

She'd shut and locked it.

Her first thought was that it could be hotel staff.

She knew that didn't fly even as she thought it. There was no reason for them to be checking her suite. The maids did the rounds in the morning and no maid visited their suite unless requested. One had yet to be requested.

Sara started to move backward, away from the suite, away from the possibility of a threat. She was being overly cautious, but considering everything that had happened, she wasn't taking a chance.

She looked at Everett and winked while mouthing *shush*. She was grateful for the silly game she'd created in the hours they'd spent alone. She had taught Everett how to play spy, and how to be extra quiet while doing so. She'd done it because of all that was happening, just in case. But to the boy it was a fun game. Now his striking, light brown eyes sparked with the anticipation of playing his new favorite game and he clamped his lips with a tiny finger on them.

She shifted him in her arms. He was almost too heavy, but she had to soldier through. She couldn't chance putting him down. Whoever had been in her room could still be there. She'd hung a Do Not Disturb sign on the door. From what she could see, it was still there. She had all her important papers with her, she always did. There was nothing for them to steal but the clothes, baby things and some cosmetics and toys that Talib had had delivered early yesterday.

Something scuffled, like a footstep sliding over paper, making it rustle, and it was coming from their suite. She remembered the newspaper that Andre had brought her earlier this morning. He had laid it on a small table by the door and only an hour ago, Everett had thrown it off. She didn't remember picking it up, she'd been distracted and...

Her thoughts broke off.

She backed up faster, smiling at Everett, being careful not to frighten him. He was still clutching an animal cracker and seemed more fascinated by the fan that turned slowly over their head than what she was frightened of. She backed away from their suite quietly and headed for the fire exit. She'd slip down that way. The elevator wasn't a thought. The last thing she needed to do was get trapped in an elevator or caught while waiting for one.

A bang behind them made her jump as it echoed down the hallway.

"Mama!" Everett squawked.

"Shh." She was terrified that they'd been heard. Terrified that whoever was in the room would be out here in seconds, threatening them, snatching her son from her arms.

She turned and ran.

"No," Everett cried as he was jostled in her arms. "Shh."

She glanced frantically over her shoulder and her worst fears were realized. There was a flash of movement, a bulky person, a man exiting their suite. There were seconds before he would see them, come after them. To her right was the fire alarm. Should she do it? It seemed rather extreme. She looked frantically behind her and now there was clearly no choice. Briefly she met the distant look of the man who was just leaving her room. It was clear now that he was wiry rather than bulky and it was also clear that he was a threat. He glared at her before he began to move in her direction. She didn't wait to see the distance between them being eaten up. She couldn't run as fast as him and carry Everett. She didn't chance another look, but swung around and pulled the fire alarm.

Chapter Nineteen

The alarm bell was ringing loudly through the hotel.

Sara fumbled with the emergency door with one arm, struggling to get it open before finally turning and ramming it open with her butt.

A door slammed to her right and she could hear excited voices.

The fire exit opened and a rush of cool air seemed to sweep around her. Compared to the opulence elsewhere, the cement and steel almost made her stop. Almost. They had to get out of here. Within a floor she was joined by others. People kept streaming in and the flow slowed with each addition. Soon she was caught in a wave of panicked people who were now moving at a crawl. Caught in the middle of the pack, she was out of sight. Everett was silently sucking his thumb. His eyes were wide, fascinated or frightened, she wasn't sure. It seemed he was more shocked than she.

She couldn't believe this was happening again. It had been a mistake to come here, to come to Morocco at all. She'd thought that she'd run away from trouble and now she only was finding herself caught in something far worse.

She shifted Everett in her arms and marveled at the fact that he was still quiet. It was the only bit of luck that was coming her way. It was up to her to keep him safe. How had she thought that it would be any other way? It had always been about her and Everett. Her son was not a responsibility she could ask anyone else to share, even Talib.

"Mama," Everett said.

"Shh." She pressed a finger to his lips.

She concentrated on keeping her footing in the crowd and putting distance between them and the intruder, and what was clearly danger targeted at her and her son. A twinge of guilt ran through her at the thought that by pulling the alarm bell she had involved not only other people, but also a whole hotel.

She'd begun the evacuation of a hotel, pulled the fire alarm when no fire existed. Behind her a woman's bag pushed into the back of her legs. She stumbled, caught her balance and reached for the railing. Her heart was pounding and her mouth was dry.

The cool stairwell was beginning to heat up from the waves of people joining at each level. Finally, they were on the main floor and bursting into the flooded lobby, where hotel staff were organizing people as they emerged. Rather than the chaos of the first hotel, this one was calm and orchestrated. No one looked anything more than slightly flustered or, in one case, put out.

She had to admit what she'd done, stop what she'd unintentionally put into motion.

She hurried over to a man with the telltale gold braid, but whose uniform indicated he might be security. He was directing people as they emerged from the stairwell. "Someone has broken into my room," she said in a hurried breath.

"We'll send someone up."

"He may be armed."

"Just a moment, madam," he said as he moved toward the desk.

"No, wait." She didn't need anyone hurt, but she needed the emergency crews called off. "I pulled the fire alarm. There is no fire."

"No fire." His eyes darkened and he picked up a phone. "You?"

"Yes," she said firmly and swallowed a ball of fear.

She was in deep trouble. She couldn't imagine what the penalty might be for a tourist falsely claiming an emergency. But there was still the threat, somewhere here in this hotel. She needed to get Everett out.

"Remain here. For the authorities." He turned to the desk and spoke rapidly, words that she didn't understand.

A voice came over the intercom, asking for calm, stating it had only been a practice run. That there was no emergency. Excited voices swirled around her.

"Don't move," the man behind the desk instructed her.

She pulled out her phone and called Talib.

No answer.

Within minutes an intercom again repeated that it had been a false alarm and promised refreshments for those remaining in the lobby. A form of compensation, she supposed. She put down Everett, never letting her hand leave his. She tried Talib again with no success. Five minutes went by and around her, the rush of the crowd was nothing like it had been in the first hotel. Instead, hotel patrons milled about chatting and laughing. Staff moved among them, offering the promised cocktails and other refreshments.

She could see a pair of men in suits. They looked big, almost bulky and definitely intimidating as they huddled together in a closed discussion. One looked up and glanced over at her.

She moved away, out of their line of vision, and sat in an overstuffed chair in the midst of a group of older, well-dressed men and women. They were chatting, enjoying their drinks and not paying much attention to her. She hoped that their numbers and loud voices might, for a minute or two, shield her.

Her eyes shifted around.

Someone had been in her room, had come after her and was more than likely still looking for her. The danger wasn't gone, at least not for her, and more importantly, not for Everett. Was the intruder connected with the hotel? He'd worn a similar jacket to hotel personnel. But there was something different in the way he had looked at her, the way he had acted. Plus, he'd worn a T-shirt beneath the jacket. That alone screamed fraud. She wasn't sure who to trust. She needed Talib desperately and she needed him now.

She remembered Talib telling her that if she sensed trouble and she couldn't, for any reason, get a hold of him, to contact his oldest brother, Emir. She had yet to follow that advice, but she hadn't been in a situation such as this. She pulled out her phone and the card he'd given her.

Emir answered with worry evident in his voice.

She frowned. That was odd. The worry was almost an omen, for it was so unlike the man she'd met, or the stories of him that Talib had told her. Something was going on but she was in no position to ask what.

"Where's Talib?" she asked shortly.

"Sara, what's wrong?" he asked instead of answering her question. His voice sounded rather stressed and there was a rush of traffic noise, a car honking in the background.

She didn't ask about any of it. She only explained what was happening.

"You were right to call me, Sara. I'll be there in five minutes. I'm actually just a few blocks away. Never mind, I'll talk to you when I get there. Stay where you are, where security can see you. And no worries, I'll handle that situation, as well."

She almost smiled at that, if smiling was even a possibility considering the circumstances. Security wasn't detaining her but she could feel their unsmiling looks burning into her. They weren't about to let her out of their sight and although it was for a different reason, that fact was oddly comforting. She put her phone into her pocket. Then she pulled out a toy car for Everett out of her other pocket. She could see two brawny security men now moving in her direction. They were well-dressed but their broad shoulders and unforgiving faces told her clearly who and what they were. But before they could reach her, the elevator doors opened and Andre rushed out.

"Madam," he said. It was the title he'd always referred to her as and it had always seemed like he was giving her the respect offered an older woman. But at twenty-five, it had seemed odd. Hearing it now was comforting. Seeing a familiar face was a relief.

"You're all right?"

"I think so. The security…"

"Won't touch you," he said. He turned to Everett and took the chubby face in his big hands and then pretended to take his nose, making the boy laugh. His dark eyes met hers. "You left the room," he said in an accusing voice.

She nodded. "There was a man leaving my room. We ran and I pulled the alarm." She didn't bother to mention her earlier infraction, the one that put them in the hallway to begin with. He didn't push the issue. She imagined with Talib she wouldn't be so lucky. But that was later.

Where was he? She picked up Everett. "Mama," he whined, struggling to get down.

She held him tighter as she turned her attention back to Andre, realizing that he was still speaking and she'd missed what he'd said. "I'm sorry. I was distracted and didn't hear what you said."

"It's all right," he replied. "I was saying that I suspected something like that when I saw you were missing. I've had the hotel locked down," he said gravely. He glanced behind them. "They know you pulled the alarm?"

She nodded.

"I'll handle it." It was a man's voice behind her. The voice was distinctive and one she'd heard only recently. She turned to see Emir and felt relief, while at the same time her heart sank. The arrival of Talib's brother only made his absence so much more noticeable. Where was Talib?

"Stay there," Emir said as he motioned to Sara. "Andre, come with me," he said in a voice that was easy and yet commanding at the same time.

Everett poked her lip with his finger and squirmed to get onto the ground. Her arms still ached from carrying him down the stairs. If Talib had been here, he'd take him from her. In such a short time, she'd gotten used to that small act of chivalry. She'd gotten used to a lot of things. She was here under the name Al-Nassar, under Talib's name, his protection, and she needed him desperately.

What would she do if she couldn't find him?

Chapter Twenty

Talib had been working the rope on his wrist, worrying it with his teeth and rubbing it back and forth on the cement edge to his right, and he was finally able to break it. He didn't consider why his attacker hadn't just killed him when he had the chance. One didn't question good luck. But the penalty for death was a lot tougher than one for assault and forcible restraint. Penalties and justice, of course, depended on one getting caught and there was no doubt in his mind that this piece of camel dung was going to get caught. Caught and tried and convicted if he had any say in it.

Bugger, he mouthed, afraid to make any sound in case there was someone above him. If he hadn't been banged up from the earlier attack, this never would have happened.

He moved his ankles, working to restore his circulation. Then something changed. He could sense that he wasn't alone.

There was a rustling above him.

That was new. There had only been silence in the time he'd been awake. How long had he been here?

He wasn't sure. He'd drifted in and out of consciousness. He was fairly certain that he'd been drugged. It was the only thing that made sense for he estimated he'd been out for hours.

It had been questionable before, the sound just a whisper, a hint of movement. Now he knew that he wasn't alone. Now there was a clear scuffing noise unique to the sound of the leather soles of traditional Moroccan shoes.

He wasn't alone. But it wasn't clear who was above him.

His attacker?

Whoever was above him, he could almost hear them breathing, as if the person was kneeling on the door that trapped him. Talib was silent. He didn't need to know he was conscious and free and ready to unleash his rage on whoever had done this to him.

Sara.

He needed to get to her. He moved his legs, quietly, clenching his fists, turning his ankles, getting the circulation going again. It was all he could do to be as quiet as possible and not break the wood above him and burst through. He would let his abductor think he still had the advantage and then take the bugger down.

Open the door, he thought, and fought his impatience.

More shuffling and then there was a thud and clunk of metal as whatever was holding the door down was shoved aside. He didn't have much time to consider what it might be before the door opened upward. Light spilled into the dark dungeon-like space he'd been trapped in. He remained still for a second, then two. He was barely breathing. His eyes were closed and every one of his senses was on alert. Then, on an inhale, he opened his eyes and bellowed a war cry meant to throw off the enemy. He lunged at his captor, moving up and out and flattening the man with the surprise of his attack and his greater size. His fist crunched the man's jaw even as his other hand sank into his midriff. In a few minutes it was over. The man was bound and thrown into the same dungeon Talib had been in. A look at the man told him that it was the same one who had accosted him in the parking lot.

Who had hired him? Had it been his old classmate? And yet none of that made sense. But there was no time for answers to any of those questions.

Urgency pulsed through him.

He remembered other things he'd heard through the hours of his captivity. Random voices that had filtered in and out as he'd struggled for consciousness. He'd heard another voice, a man's, and a mention of the Sahara Sunset. More than one man was involved in this and he'd only trapped one. Worse, they knew the name of the hotel where Sara and his son were staying.

Sara's safe place had been compromised.

He pulled a cell phone from the man's pocket. This piece of filth would be under lock and key within the hour and not just the makeshift one that Talib had tossed him into.

"Have a nice life," he said sarcastically as he slid the metal rod across the door, locking the unconscious man inside. It was two o'clock in the afternoon. He'd been held captive much longer than he thought.

He emerged out of what had only been a shanty of a room in the basement of the apartment building he'd so recently visited. He limped down the narrow corridor and burst out into a silent alley. The circulation in his legs was coming back, in tingles that made his gait more unsteady than smooth. But he didn't have time to think about that. He needed to get to Sara and the boy.

"Where are you?" Emir asked as he took the call from Talib.

"Not relevant," Talib said shortly, thinking of the hours he'd been held captive. How much time had passed? His watch was gone, so was his gun.

"Very relevant, Talib. What the hell is going on?"

"Surprise attack. I'm okay," he said before Emir could ask about his well-being. He could feel the sweat on his forehead. It seemed like it had taken forever to get here, to where he had parked the car. He was lucky to be alive, he knew that. But he had more important things to concern himself with. He needed to make sure Sara and the boy remained safe. "Look, we have a situation. I need to get Sara and the boy out of that hotel and to the compound as quickly as possible. I have one of our suspects restrained." He gave him the location and briefly told him what had transpired.

"We need to get a tail on Habib Kattanni. I went to school with him as a kid. Family went hard up and somehow it seems he's involved in this. We need to know where he is and what he's doing now."

"I'll handle it," Emir said. "In the meantime, there's a situation at the Sahara Sunset."

"What the…" He broke off, already running in a limping gait for his vehicle.

"Fire alarm went off. There was no fire."

"No fire. Sara and the boy?"

"Sara pulled the alarm, T." Emir went on to explain what had happened. "I'm at the hotel with Sara now."

"He was there. I know it."

"Who?"

"Habib. I'll be there in ten, can you wait?"

"I'm not following, but yeah, I'm not going anywhere."

Talib moved out of the silent alley and into the noise and congestion of the souk. The narrow, walled corridor was filled with people, merchants and chaos. To think he'd been trapped so close to all this was ludicrous. To think he'd been attacked at all again, and by who—unthinkable.

Somehow his school days, which he had once remembered as a time of innocence, now seemed a breeding ground for one boy to turn to corruption and evil. And now that evil threatened his family.

He blinked. The light hurt his eyes.

And he didn't consider how the idea of family had so quickly and easily evolved to include Sara and Everett.

Sara waited as Emir spoke to the hotel officials. Andre stood like a shadow to her right, not letting them out of his sight, and somehow his stoic presence only reminded her of the mess her life was in. Then she saw Talib striding through the front entrance. She hurried toward him. But she was stopped as a security officer seemed to emerge from the shadows and placed a hand on her upper arm. He was followed by a second security officer.

"Ma'am, a word," the shorter of the two said, but what he lacked in height he made up for in muscular girth.

"Please, I..."

"Let her go," Emir's cool voice demanded beside her.

Andre stood just behind him, his silent and equally intimidating presence backing him up.

Everett slipped and she would have dropped him, but strong hands had him out of her arms and she was face-to-face with Talib.

"Yes, I'm sorry, Mr. Al-Nassar."

The security team looked at the two brothers, who now flanked Sara. The men eased back, each gave a small bow and they moved away.

Everett took that moment to begin to snuffle, his face red and clearly ready to launch into something more epic. Talib put a finger on his lips and offered him a smile, which seemed to calm him.

"Are you all right?" Talib asked with a look of concern that made her want to sink into his arms. Her hands shook and her head ached and she looked up at him with relief. But that relief disappeared when she saw his face. He'd been banged up before but now he was much worse. One side of his face was entirely black and blue and he seemed to favor his left arm as if it was in pain. His hair was dull with what looked like dirt. All in all he was a mess, not the pulled-together man she knew. It was only the determined look in his eyes and the proud stance that was the same. Otherwise he looked like he'd been to hell and back.

"What happened?"

"It's not important," he growled.

"You were beat up," she persisted. "What happened? Where have you been?" she asked, not meaning to sound accusatory.

"I was in a situation or two," he said with a smile.

She couldn't help herself, her finger ran along his cheek. There was something more, something he was hiding. "What aren't you telling me?"

"Let's just say for now that I was broadsided, unexpectedly. I expect now, he looks worse than I do," Talib replied.

"You're sure? That you're okay," she said.

"I'm fine." His left arm was around her waist as he held their son in the crook of his other arm.

"Talib?" Emir said. "I don't mean to interrupt but we need to get some things sorted out."

"Wait here with Andre," he said to her and strode after his brother.

Sara sank down into a nearby chair, ignoring the big man by her side, her gaze following Talib as he walked away with Everett. The three were similar in so many ways, two men and a boy—family.

Something caught in her throat. Already, it had begun.

Chapter Twenty-One

"Where have you been?" Emir asked. "What happened?" he added before Talib could say anything to the first question. "Details this time."

"I was broadsided. I can't believe this, the second time…"

"Same unsub?"

"The one I've detained, yes. He's not going anywhere."

Emir nodded. "I didn't get a chance between your call and Sara's but I'll get the authorities on it."

"I was jumped from behind, thrown into a storage area that was hidden beneath the floorboards and left. I didn't get a visual on that one but I'm assuming it's the same guy. At some point, I heard him talking to another man. Don't know who he was. But before that I found a name on a scrap of paper. Here's where it gets strange. Like I told you earlier, I went to primary school with this guy. The guy whose name was on the paper. Like he was some kind of contact. I'm not sure what the connection was."

"Son of a…" Emir shook his head. "I was worried, I never thought—"

"But you were going after me," Talib interrupted as he eyed the bulletproof vest.

"Of course," Emir said.

"I'll get the other situation, your man in the cellar, cleaned up." Emir looked over at Sara. "In the meantime, we need to get Sara out of here. As you said, the man behind all this knows she's here. And you and me need to talk. I've got the office on alert, this case is moving to code red."

They looked at each other, both of them knowing that a code red meant their agent needed backup. It was the most dangerous case, unlike white, which was the one least fraught with danger.

"I think it's contained," Talib said. "At least in the short term, if we can get Sara and the boy to the compound they'll be safe. At least for now."

FIVE MINUTES LATER the head of security shook Talib's hand. "This breach in security is troubling. We've checked camera footage and it appears there was an intruder. He slipped in through a delivery entrance. This has never happened before." He shook his head. "He's left the building. We've verified that and we are in the process of beefing up the defective area. That doesn't change what happened." He looked at Sara. "I'm so sorry. We pride ourselves on the safety of our hotel. Can we offer you an upgraded suite or…"

She shook her head. "No, thank you." She couldn't

imagine anything more luxurious than what she already had.

More effusive apologies went on before it was only the three of them.

"What happened, Sara?" Talib asked. "I know you told me the short version but I don't understand, I mean I got how he came in, but you weren't in the room. How did he know that? Was he watching?"

She shook her head. "I don't know any of that. I'm just glad we weren't there. I don't think he expected us back so soon." She looked at him. "He could have planned to hide in the suite and take Everett."

He didn't mention that there was no need to hide. He only needed to overpower Sara, not a difficult feat. A chill ran through him at the thought.

"Why did you leave the room, Sara?"

She shook her head. "Everett was bored. We were both going stir-crazy."

"That's no excuse. You could have taken Andre."

"I thought it was safe. It's not Andre's fault," she said quickly. "I slipped out, it was stupid."

"Beyond foolhardy," he said darkly. "Promise me you won't do anything like that again."

"I promise."

He put his palms on either side of her face and leaned down and kissed her. "If something had happened to you…" He looked over at Everett. "Or him. I don't know what I would have done." He pulled her down onto one of the lobby couches. "Tell me what happened."

"When I realized that there was someone there

and that they might come after us, I knew I had to do something. So I pulled the alarm when it looked like he had seen us. We were going to head down the emergency exit and he—he..." She stopped as if to catch her breath, gather her thoughts. "He was headed toward us. All things considered..."

"You're out of here." He hadn't meant to present the idea so bluntly. That was how he spoke to his brothers but this was Sara, the woman he... His thoughts broke off.

"What do you mean?"

He could see the panic run through her in the way her face went from pale to white.

"You're walking?" she asked in a small voice.

"Walking? What are you talking about?"

"I know we're in trouble and..."

"You think I'm washing my hands of you?"

She nodded.

"Are you out of your mind? I didn't say I was out of here," he said with disbelief. "I said you're out of here. And I meant you'll be going with me." Leaving her was the last thing on his mind. Leaving his son, never. "There's no choice now, you need to go to the family compound, where we can control access. I don't want—"

"You're getting no arguments from me," she interrupted in a voice filled with relief. "Let's go." And with a frown that seemed as much pained as determined.

"We'll end this," he said with gritted teeth, conscious of the boy in his arms.

"Let's go," Sara repeated as she slipped her hand tentatively into his.

And it was with that simple gesture that his decision was made. It was time to play hard ball.

Chapter Twenty-Two

The elevator door opened on the ninth floor.

Sara looked up at Talib. He could see the relief in her eyes. They both knew that after all that had happened she couldn't stay here another night.

"You can't stay here. The Nassar family compound isn't so bad," he said as he followed her out into the spacious hall.

"Just get us to safety," she said in a hoarse whisper. "I won't argue. And with any luck I won't be running…"

"You won't have to run from anyone ever again," he interrupted.

"I knew this was no life to live even before I got on that plane."

"You should have got on that plane a lot sooner than you did," he said.

"I know," she whispered.

"You'll be safer at the compound. Until we get this thing sorted out." He looked down and pushed a curl of hair off his son's face. "I planned to move you there first thing in the morning. Now I don't have to convince you."

"I know there's no choice," she said. "I wish there was…"

"The game has shifted players and the last thing I need to be doing is worrying about you," Talib said.

She looked at him with a frown.

There were so many things unspoken in that sentence. For by refusing to go to the compound, he knew that she blamed herself for his attack. She'd said as much.

He went to put his arm around her shoulders and winced as pain shot through his injured arm.

"I'm so sorry, Talib. It's my fault."

"It's not your fault, you did what you thought was best."

She shook her head. "No. Going there, to your family's compound. It wffas like a line in the sand. I couldn't do it. I thought I'd lose Everett to you and going there sealed the deal."

"Me?"

"The Al-Nassars." She wiped her eyes with the back of her hand. "I should have realized sooner that none of that mattered as long as he's safe."

"He's safe and no one is taking him from you, Sara. You're his mother. You'll always be his mother."

She looked up at him with gratitude and something else shining in her eyes. He didn't want to acknowledge what that might be for it frightened him and she looked away so quickly he thought he might have imagined it. It was a look that said that he was still her everything. Maybe that was only what he wanted to see. He pushed the thoughts away.

Instead, he thought of telling her about Tad. That he was dead and she didn't have to worry about him, but something stopped him. It was a time crunch and Tad's death didn't eliminate the threat to her. He needed to get moving, put a stop to this. And the other reason was he didn't want her to let down her guard. He'd rather have her vigilant and worried than… He couldn't think of the alternative.

"Damn," he said as he swung around. He needed to tell her. It wasn't fair otherwise.

"What's going on, Talib?" Sara asked, reading the look on his face like she seemed to do so easily. "Whatever it is, I need to know," she said softly.

She was right. She was strong enough to handle anything. She'd handled months on the run, raised a baby by herself and kept the two of them from starving. She'd done a lot before she'd come to him.

"Sit down," he said softly, directing her to a set of chairs in an alcove near her room. He'd held this news to himself for too long. It was time that she knew that the originator of this horror was no longer a threat.

"That bad?" she asked, but she sat.

"Tad Rossi was arrested in the States on assault charges. He ripped off an elderly lady at an ATM."

She put her hand to her mouth, her eyes horrified.

"I don't know how to put this. There's no way to soften it."

"Just say it," she said.

"He died in police custody."

Silence sat heavily between them. Her lips were parted and her wide gray eyes were shocked. She didn't move, it was almost as if she couldn't breathe.

He hugged her with his free arm. The embrace was brief.

"It's not over, remember that," he said. "I need you to be vigilant. Promise me."

"I promise," she whispered, but there was the first hint of a real smile on her face.

"We'll get your luggage collected and delivered to the compound." He put his free hand on her shoulder. She felt so small, so fragile. And then she looked up at him and concern was in her eyes and the way she ran her finger gently down one bruised cheek.

"You got this protecting us."

There was no answer to that statement. It was true and he knew he would do it again. "If they breach those defenses, it'll be the last thing they breach," he said ominously. "No worries. There isn't a safer place in the city, or even the country."

"I know," she said softly. "It's why I'm here. I was just afraid."

He looked at her as Everett ran his thumb along his earlobe as if that was normal, as if he'd done it forever. The soft feel of that tentative touch as if the boy was making sure he was real made it hard to focus on what was important.

She stood up.

He followed.

He looked at Sara and saw tears in her eyes.

His hand was on her waist. "You're okay?" he asked.

She backed up.

"You're afraid? No one will hurt you. You know that."

She shook her head. "I do know that. I'm sorry, Talib I'm just…"

Shock ran through him. "You're afraid of me. Is that it?" He couldn't believe it. "You're his mother, Sara. Nothing will change that. I just want a chance to know him and be his father."

She smiled but the smile didn't quite meet her eyes.

"Wait here. I'll make sure the room is clear."

A few minutes later he emerged from the suite. "It's safe. Get what you need and let's get out of here."

She headed into the suite, looking back once, and he gave her a smile of encouragement but turned almost immediately to his phone. There was work that needed to be done and he was learning to do it one-handed with his son in his other arm. He needed to put the pieces in place that would keep them safe. Whether she knew it or not, this was no longer her game. It never had been—it was his.

"THIS HAS NEVER been anything but personal," Talib said with a low growl in his throat. "He wants money and he wants to bring our family down."

"He's become more resourceful over the years," Emir said. "From two-bit crime to possible kidnapping—"

"Never going to happen," Talib interrupted.

"We know that," Emir said impatiently. "As I was saying he's evolved to kidnapping and blackmail."

"On our side he may be more desperate," Talib said. "From what we've discovered when he was contacted by Sara's ex, he saw a cash cow."

"The ex is gone and Habib has lost many of his men. Poor planning on Habib's part, it seems everything was just dashed together. So now we have a desperate man ready to do anything. Is he still in Marrakech?"

"There's no guarantees. The only thing we know for sure is that he didn't take any kind of public transport out of the city. I'll get Sara settled in Tara's suite at the compound."

"He's smart enough not to rent anything in his own name."

"You're right about that," Talib agreed. "I'll get research to run some aliases."

"That's not enough."

"I know," Talib agreed. "I've put in an order to get a paper trail that takes Sara and the boy back to the States. With any luck, he follows that and the police can make an arrest."

"And if not," Emir said, "Kate and I are out of town on the weekend. There's no getting around it. A friend of Kate's from Montreal is getting married here in Morocco. They're both geologists and are fascinated by the Sahara. Anyway," he said with a look of concern, "we're the only witnesses. But I think we have time. And our new hire, Khalid, is just off his first assignment. Don't hesitate to use him."

"I'll be fine, Emir. I'm a professional."

"Watch your back T, and don't get cocky."

Talib rubbed the back of his neck. "I think I learned that lesson a few hours ago."

Chapter Twenty-Three

Talib was on his phone again when Sara returned, his other arm holding their son, who was smiling and pulling his father's earlobe.

He disconnected and asked what had been taken.

"Nothing," she said. "I'm packed and ready to go." The clothes she had were all new, purchased and delivered in the hours when she'd first arrived at the hotel by someone in Talib's office. Like Everett's toys, everything had arrived without her mentioning the need.

He looked at his phone as if considering what he should or should not reveal.

"What's up?" she asked.

"The police arrested the suspect two blocks from the hotel. Looks like he slipped in while a delivery was being made. Hotel security is all over that breach."

"Who was it?"

"Not who I expected," he said bluntly.

She stopped and turned to face him. "Who did you expect?"

"I know who is behind this," he said. "It wasn't him, but we'll stop him before this happens again."

Everett was clinging to Talib's pant leg and chortling as Talib shook his leg slightly, making his son cling harder and laugh.

"You're not telling me everything," she said. "Including what really happened to you." She was quiet for a moment. "You'll tell me when this is all over?"

"Promise," he said, his attention focused on her despite his leg antics for his son. "I promise I'll tell you a lot of things when this is all over. All of them good."

He bent to kiss her. She hadn't expected that and she didn't pull away and couldn't as his lips parted hers and she only wanted to melt into him. But he'd always had that effect on her.

She took a step back.

"No, Talib. Not now." What was she saying? Not ever. But she wasn't so sure about that. She wanted Talib. She always had and that was where the problems had all begun.

"Leave the bags. They'll be picked up and loaded before we get downstairs," Talib assured her.

She looked at him and one thought seemed to overwhelm her. The return date on her airline ticket was burned into her memory, but Everett didn't have to go home. It was unthinkable and yet he'd be safe. She turned away as tears burned her eyes.

"Sara." He had his hands on her shoulders as he turned her to look at him. "It will be all right. I'll find the bugger and he'll pay. No one will hurt you again."

She clung to his last statement and hoped against

hope that the "no one" he referred to included himself. And she never told him the other fear, the dread that ran deep and aching through her being. It was nothing she could fix and something she had to learn to live with—life without Everett.

Talib picked up Everett and said something that made the boy laugh. A bellhop waited with a cart to take their bags and within minutes they were in the main lobby. The lobby had returned to calm elegance. The chaos of the earlier alarm had been quickly swept away and only cultured sophistication remained.

"I'm going to miss it here," Sara said with a laugh. "My last stay in high-end luxury. Wave goodbye, Ev," she said, but pain clutched her heart at the thought that it was more than likely not her son's last stay in such luxury. For him, it was only beginning. And while it made her happy to know he'd have opportunities she'd never know, it was the thought of letting him go so he had that chance that was killing her.

"You may be surprised," Talib said dryly.

"Are you suggesting more luxury?" she said with a teasing note in her voice despite her pain.

"Much more," he replied.

Five minutes later they were making their way through Marrakech. The hotel had been on the edge of the Medina. It was where the tourists flocked for a taste of exotica, to barter in the souks and soak up the culture. It was where the locals came to get the necessities of day-to-day life. Within minutes, they were on a busy freeway. High-rise buildings, both commercial property and penthouse apartments, bor-

dered the freeway. To her, Marrakech was just another city and she'd seen too many in recent months.

She looked back where Everett was secured into a
brand-new car seat. She glanced at Talib. His attention was on the road, but there was a small quirk to
his full lips, like he was smiling.

"You're happy?"

"Relieved," he said and he glanced at her before
returning his attention to the road. "The two of you
are safe and I can focus on getting this threat behind bars."

Again, guilt washed over her. It had been her stubbornness, her need to have her son to herself and her
fear that had drawn this out longer than it ever needed
to be. She should have told Talib the truth months ago.

"I'm sorry this happened while you were under my
protection. I should have been there…"

"You were investigating, finding the threat. Who
else would do that if not you?" To her, the question
was only proof that no apology was necessary.

"Still, it was my fault, if I had been there—"

"No, it was mine," she insisted. "If anyone broadsided anyone, it was me with the news of Everett.
You weren't on your game and it was my fault. I'm
sorry. If I hadn't overwhelmed you, you might have
been more prepared, and the attacker wouldn't have
injured you like he did."

"Ouch," he said. "You're also psychic?"

"I didn't mean that in a derogatory way," she said
softly. "You're everything I've always known you to

be and more. I wouldn't have come here otherwise. There's no one more qualified to protect our son."

He looked at her with surprise in his eyes and something seemed to soften in his face. But he didn't say anything about her pronouncement. Instead he returned his attention to the road as a comfortable silence settled between them.

"I'm sorry I've been so much trouble. You'll be relieved when we leave."

"Leave…" The word trailed off as if he'd never considered the possibility.

"Our flight home," she replied, dodging her earlier thoughts about leaving her son. It was a consideration that no mother wanted to contemplate and not one she wanted to admit yet. "It seems trouble has only followed us here. We may be safer at home now with Tad gone."

"No."

"No?"

"Definitely not," he said.

And they drove the rest of the way in silence, both of them deep in their own thoughts.

Chapter Twenty-Four

Sara was glad for her son's silence. It gave her a chance to take in the full effect of the Al-Nassar estate, to let the opulence sink into her reality. It was majestic. The grounds alone were overwhelming. She could only imagine the mansion, which sprawled in the distance. Palm trees lined the drive and on the left she could see the beginning of a glistening infinity pool. The city of Marrakech seemed to have faded into the background, even though Talib had assured her that the compound was well within city limits.

"It's huge," she breathed. They'd just passed through a security check, a one-roomed stucco cabin that was just at the entrance. At that gate, Talib conversed with a middle-aged man with a rock-hard physique and an equally intimidating AK-47 over his shoulder. The conversation ended and the iron gates opened and they moved on.

"Five acres," he replied. "We've beefed up security. There are cameras 24/7."

"Everywhere?" she said in a voice that sounded small.

"Inside and out."

"You expect trouble?" she asked and her voice sounded worried even to her.

"We upped the security for exactly the opposite reason. To prevent trouble," he said. "You're safe here. Safer than the hotel and definitely safer than on your own in the States. There are sensors in the wall monitoring activity on either side of the wall."

Her eyes followed the sweep of his arm, where a cream-colored masonry fence surrounded the entire complex. She knew about some of the high-profile cases Nassar Security handled from what Talib had told her when they were dating. Between that and the family wealth, security was a priority. Ironically, it was security that they'd founded their business on.

She nodded. She could only hope that he was right. But she'd placed her trust in him and so far, despite the threats, he'd done just that—protect them. But seeing this, his family's home, only confirmed what she already knew. He was out of her league. He proved it now and he'd proved it before. And he always had been. Maybe that was why the romance had faded, at least for him.

Their lives were polar opposites. This was the life that Everett would inherit. This world wasn't hers. Things would change, she knew that. She'd have to learn, at worst, to share Everett. He was no longer a secret and deep in her heart she knew that he never should have been. But she wasn't ready to admit that, not now—possibly never.

Because of Everett they had to find common ground to make him a home where their differences equated only to a shared love for him. It was a lot to think about for a woman who'd only celebrated her quarter-century birthday three months ago. But since she'd become pregnant with Everett, she'd grown up fast. She'd set her mind with the same dedication she had to her career, to parenting her son.

She looked around, admiring the grounds as if she was a tourist dropped into an opulent resort. His world. So very different from hers. They'd just passed four men with guns strapped across their backs. Now they were passing a more bucolic scene.

No guns, no Tad to worry about, just a peaceful and luxurious landscape. The endless sweep of emerald-green lawn, the elegant curve of the drive all fronted the massive home in front of them. She couldn't believe it was almost over. In her mind it was, it was only Talib that wanted to make extra sure.

She folded her hands together, glanced back at Everett, saw that his attention was caught by something and relaxed. He was safe and a good part of the trouble had shifted to Talib's shoulders. She felt guilty at the relief that ran through her, but she'd carried the load alone for so long. She also felt guilty about being relieved about a man's death. But that's all she felt about the demise of Tad. In fact, knowing he was gone almost made her smile. That was so wrong and yet her world now felt so right. She had Everett and Talib together, at least for a time. It was heaven. Or at least she could pretend it was so. She glanced over at Talib. She didn't delude herself, what she felt for him wasn't what he felt for her. She knew that. She loved him, she always had.

Talib braked for a peacock that strolled across the road. "Darn, I wish they'd keep those things contained." He glanced over at her. "Tara's idea," he said. "We have three of them. Noisier than hell at odd times of the day."

"Beautiful," she said with a smile. The bird's vibrant feathers were folded in as he moved along the side of the road and over to where a hedge was manicured into the shape of a small pyramid.

"The hedges?" she asked, wondering which of his siblings had come up with the idea and knowing it wasn't Talib.

"Emir's idea," he said. "Seems my siblings are turning this place into the Al-Nassar Disneyland."

She smiled.

Two minutes later, they got out of the car at the entrance of the mansion that stretched out on either side of them. The white tiled entrance gleamed. Soaring white columns rose on either side of a massive, arched set of doors. It was opulence on a level she'd never seen.

Inside was every bit as awe-inspiring as the outside. Twenty-foot-high ceilings stretched out on either side. White columns like those outside, only slimmer, more elegant, ran the length of the hall. The ivory-colored, tiled floor seemed to wink in the well-lit vastness that stretched endlessly in front of them. She'd never seen anything like this. Even Everett was quiet as if he, too, was overwhelmed by the size and scale of everything.

The pictures of ancestors dating back generations, lined one part of the expansive wall. All of it was luxury like she had only glimpsed at the hotel. This was so much more. This was a side of Talib she hadn't known. She knew that he was wealthy. She knew that he had the resources to save their son, but she'd never quantified what exactly that might mean.

Ten minutes later they stood outside one of the largest doors she'd ever seen in the interior of any home. A heart insignia made from what looked like gold was on the panel of each door.

He looked back at her with an impish smile. "The old harem quarters."

"Talib," she giggled, and for the first time there was a lighthearted humor between them like there had been when they first dated.

"Tara's apartment," he said with a smile. "She got a laugh out of living in the harem, but she's done it all up so it doesn't look anything like the old days."

"I think I'd like your sister," she said quietly.

"She'll be here in a few months for a break."

In a few months she herself would be long gone, she thought, and wondered if he'd just realized the same.

"It's where you'll be safest," he said as he turned to look at her. "Tara no longer stays here much. You'll be secure here and there's a suite just over there." He pointed just behind them and to her left, where a smaller door was almost hidden. "Servants used to stay there," he said with a grin. "I'll be staying there. It's not far away from your suite. In fact it's just out the door and to your right. You'll be safe."

She skated over the safe part, caught on the luxury he was showing her. "Me?" She stopped in the middle of the doorway. "Here?"

"You," HE SAID CONFIDENTLY. "Like I said, I'll be nearby. I'm not leaving you alone. Not again." He looked at her in a way that made her want to melt. "It's safe here and until this thing is resolved, I won't be leaving you for any length of time. Estate security will be on extra alert."

He turned his back to her as he entered the code and the majestic doors opened in effortless silence.

"State-of-the-art electronics," Talib said with a shrug. He pulled a key out of his pocket as a smaller door was revealed.

"Extra security," he said as he unlocked it the old-fashioned way.

Inside, the apartment was sleek and modern, like the penthouse apartments she'd seen on television.

The ivory tile that had been in the hallway continued into the suite.

She walked through the gleaming kitchen to a sitting area that looked out onto the expansive infinity pool. Palm trees moved gently in a breeze that had come up as the afternoon waned.

"Wow." It was all she could think to say.

She moved around the kitchen to where a sitting area with a wall-length bookcase was offset by a soft leather yellow sofa. She thought of Everett and gri-maced. To her left was a teak desk that looked well-worn and loved.

"There's plenty to keep me entertained anyway," she said. She scanned the eclectic collection of books, including a row of children's books, from picture books to classics. She wondered if that had been a new addition, put there for Everett.

He looked at Sara. "You'll be safe here," he said. "That's the important thing."

His phone beeped.

"I need to take this." He held up his hand. "Just a minute."

"CAN YOU MEET me at my office?" Ian said. "The maid who returned Sara Elliott's son is scheduled to work this evening."

"And you think she'll show up?" He realized there was a big chunk of information that Ian didn't know and he wasn't about to fill him in. At least not yet.

"Fifteen minutes. Can you be here?"

"I won't miss it," he said dryly as he thought of the bouts of bad luck he'd had with the other suspects.

"Listen, sweetheart," he said a few minutes later as he held both of Sara's hands in his. "I've got a lead on getting this resolved. I won't be gone long. You'll be safe here and if you need anything just buzz. There's an army of servants and a security team that would make your White House proud. Don't leave the apartment."

She laughed and squeezed his hands. "We'll be fine. Ev is napping and I'll just read a book."

Ten minutes later he was in Ian's office and a minute after that they had confirmation that the maid had shown up. They weren't the only ones waiting for her—a plainclothes police office was also on site waiting to interview the woman.

In fact, it was the police officer who escorted the frightened woman into their office. It wasn't very long before it was clear that other than a description of the man who'd contracted her, there wasn't much she could tell them.

But from the description it was clear, at least to Talib, that the suspect who was in collusion with her was not Habib nor was it the man he had disabled a few hours ago.

In the end, the maid told them not much more than they already knew. That aside, she wasn't free to leave, either. She was still an accessory to an attempted kidnapping and was taken into custody. Talib felt for her, but even his influence couldn't change the course of justice.

Chapter Twenty-Five

Talib made sure that the estate was locked down and that Sara and the boy had everything they needed before retiring to his own suite of rooms.

He'd returned early enough to order their supper and give Sara a rundown on how things worked. He had to smile at how blown away she was at the idea of having three servants at her beck and call. And by the fact that she didn't need to prepare a single meal, despite a kitchen that any chef would die for.

But that bit of lightheartedness aside, his thoughts were on more life-and-death things. He'd thought of arming Sara, just in case, but when he mentioned that alternative her face had turned white. He'd immediately backpedaled on that suggestion. He hadn't realized what a pacifist she was. The subject had never come up while they were dating.

There were many things he hadn't realized about her, but he was learning quickly. His ex-girlfriend, the mother of his son, was deeper than he'd ever imagined in those long ago days of going out. Then it had only been about the fun and the passion. Now it was about reality and a threat that should be part of no one's reality. But all Al-Nassars were familiar with threats. Wealth was a siren call that attracted the opportunists, a double-edged sword that the family had wrestled with over the years.

He'd told Sara to stay inside for the next day at least, as at the hotel, and she'd agreed. Unlike the hotel, this time he was sure she'd follow up on her promise. She'd learned the hard truth of safety breach consequences. He'd assured her that it wouldn't be for long. There were upgrades to the security that needed to be done and he planned to get them done by the end of the next day.

Sara.

She was exceptional. He couldn't ask for a better mother for his son. Yet, a streak of anger and even of hurt ran through him at the thought that only desperation had allowed her to trust him. Only desperation had given him his son.

The next morning, he stopped to check on them before heading out for the day. It was time to get some answers. Already the police would have finished their interrogation and he wanted to hear what they'd learned.

Twenty minutes later he was in police headquarters. He strode past the counter and through a door made to stop anyone not in uniform. But he wasn't just anyone. His family name opened doors—combined with his reputation, he knew, with no degree of false pride, that no one in this building would stop him.

He reached his destination on the second floor and entered a large, rather sparse office.

"Talib." Diwan Zidan was a large man with a rich chocolate complexion who stood a quarter of an inch taller than Talib's six foot three. Now he rose and held out his hand, leaning across his desk and smiling an undeniable welcome. "It's been a long time."

Diwan was a detective Talib had worked with often. Despite the problems in the police force, he was among a select few that Talib trusted completely. Over the years they'd shared tips, one helping the other to close cases. It was an informal relationship, a friendship that had begun with their fathers and moved to the sons. Unfortunately, both their fathers had died too early. Both in what were originally labeled traffic accidents. Diwan's father's death had been an accident. His parents' accident, and resulting deaths, had unfortunately not been. That had been a long time ago. But it had changed the family's world.

"It's been a while."

"Thank the stars for that. Every time I see you it's bad news," Diwan said with a smile, before looking down at his computer. He then scrolled through what was on the screen. "I assume you're here because of what happened at the Desert Sands Hotel."

"You've had your ear to the ground," Talib said with a chuckle.

"My job," he said shortly. "You were attacked twice by the same man." He shook his head. "Hard to believe that one."

"I'm pretty banged up," Talib said in his own defense.

"I've seen you look better." He pulled out a file.

"The maid wasn't able to give us any information. She was exactly as you thought, an opportunist who had a change of heart." He gestured to a chair on the other side of his desk. "Have a seat."

He opened the file and pulled out a picture, turning it around so Talib could see. It was a picture of a thirtysomething man with a sullen expression.

"The guy who attacked you." He looked up. "Twice."

Talib bit back a scathing remark birthed out of his own embarrassment.

"Just a small-time crook. We've got him in a holding cell. He's refusing to talk." He sat down before continuing. "We brought him in and had him interrogated by one of our female investigators. Sometimes that's more effective than men." He shook his head. "Not in this case, though. He was still pretty tight-lipped but he did give us the name of the man who contracted him. Here's where it gets interesting. The man who contracted him knows you, Talib. Not just knows of you, but there's a family connection." He opened another file and pulled out an old newspaper article. "Back in the day, before most things were online, his family made headlines."

Talib looked and saw a face that rang a bell, but didn't bring anything immediately to mind. But he knew who Diwan was going to say. Coming here today was only adding to what he already knew.

"He went to the same primary school as you, same class. Wealthy family. Scandal involving gambling on borrowed funds and some suspicious stock market trades." He looked up. "But you know this?"

"Some of it," Talib admitted.

"The family left Morocco over fifteen years ago."

"And fast-forward to today," Talib said impatiently. He was trying to move the story along.

But Diwan had a love of telling a story and when he had a handle on a good one, he wasn't about to be hurried.

"Not quite, my impatient friend. So you remember him, Habib Kattanni?"

Talib nodded. "The question is how did he hook up with Sara Elliott's ex-boyfriend?"

"Tad went to public school with him. When Sara came here I'm betting he panicked. He needed help fast. Who better then Habib, a small-time crook he was once friends with who is living in Marrakech to help regain control of Sara? Especially with the ante upped—I mean your family's wealth and all."

"Son of a…" Talib's curse broke off as his fists clenched.

"There's no known address on Habib. Wherever he's living, he's keeping low. We'll get a report filed on him and hopefully he'll be picked up."

They looked at each other and neither said what they were thinking, but it was clear that they both had the same thoughts. That he was more violent and unpredictable now as his resources ran out.

"Watch your back, Talib," Diwan said. "I'd send some extra men your way, but with the recent attacks on the outskirts of the city and a flu bug running through the ranks, I'm low on men. Anyway, Habib has made a relatively successful life of crime. He's the one you need to watch, Talib. The others were disposable."

Talib shook his head. Everything he'd heard was typical of so many career criminals.

They shook hands and four minutes later he was back in the BMW heading for home and Sara.

HABIB KATTANNI NEVER thought that Al-Nassar would get away. He should have guessed that he would. The family lived on luck. It didn't matter what tragedy they had to deal with. They came out smelling sweet. They always had.

He hated them and he hated Talib the most. But none of that mattered. What mattered was getting the money. He'd been an idiot. He'd tried for revenge and he'd failed. Talib had gotten away. He wasn't sure how, but he had. If he was here he'd kill him with his bare hands.

He gritted his teeth. That was impossible, he knew that. Without an advantage, Talib could take him down in an instant and had on that horrible day in primary school when they'd both been ten years old. It had been one of the most humiliating experiences of his life. The worst had happened the next day, when his father had publicly declared his bankruptcy. He'd been removed from the school where other children of wealth and privilege went. Al-Nassar had given him a bloody lip when he was a boy and he'd set his life for failure ever since.

Now he had a chance to put his life back together and get the final revenge. This time when he took the boy, he'd make sure that no one ever saw the little brat again. This time it wasn't Talib Al-Nassar he vowed would die, but his son.

He'd hired out with his last attempt at the Desert Sands and two of his hires had been caught. The other had blown the simple job he'd been hired for and hadn't been heard from since. But Habib wasn't in the business of being screwed around. He'd had to step in himself, it was the only way to get the job done.

The only thing that had been accomplished at the hotel was to frighten the woman. She wouldn't be staying there a moment longer. It was the only logical move, to get her out of there and take her and the boy to the safest place possible. There was only one place safer than a hotel that housed royalty and that was the Al-Nassar estate or compound, as they'd always called it. He'd hated the term. He'd hated everything about them.

They thought it was so safe, so impenetrable. And it was. Not just anyone could breach the well-protected grounds. But he wasn't just anyone.

He had an in that they wouldn't expect. He had friends in all kinds of places and it was about time he looked up the one he had at the Office National de l'Electricité. He was sure something could be arranged to let him slip by the security, it didn't have to be a long power outage, just one at the right time.

Chapter Twenty-Six

"I've bad news, Sara. You were right in assuming that Tad had connected with someone here," Talib said. "You might want to sit."

She looked reluctant but sat on the edge of the sofa just off the dining area. She laced her fingers together, her hands on her lap. "Tell me."

"The little worm he's hooked up with went to primary school with me. It was only for a few years. I wouldn't remember him except there was a scandal and his parents pulled him out." The memory of that for a moment diverted his anger. "I remember they moved. I never considered where they would have gone."

"Go on."

"The game has changed, Sara. We've found out a few things that surprise and concern me. Appears your boyfriend…" He wasn't sure why he tagged that on, but he knew it pissed her off like nothing else he could say would. Unless, of course, he said something derogatory about the boy. But he would never do that, couldn't… The boy was perfect in the way that only one's child can be.

"He's not—"

"No matter," he said, cutting her off even though he knew he'd said it that way to anger her. It was stupid. One of the childish things one does in a relationship to provoke the other. In this situation it was uncalled for because for one, they weren't in a relationship. "I'm sorry," he said and he truly meant it. He had to get his emotions under control.

"I only remember him, the man Tad partnered with, because at the time, what happened to Habib's family was so dramatic that the adults talked about it in front of us."

"What happened?"

"Bankruptcy," he said, the word stark and as bare as its meaning.

"You remember things like that," she agreed softly with a troubled look on her face.

"His family lost everything in the stock market crash. His father unwisely invested everything, diversified too little, probably trying to recoup prior losses. Instead they went from wealth to selling their properties in order to survive. They emigrated to England. After that, I heard nothing…" He made a note of another line of investigation that needed to be followed. "Apparently he's back and has been for a while. He also leans toward petty theft and a lot of unsavory acquaintances, but other than a couple of brushes with the law he's a free man."

"So what's changed?" Sara asked, a puzzled expression on her face.

"Since Tad contacted him he's hooked up with some other unsavory types. He was responsible for ramping up the kidnapping threats. The others are in custody." He covered her hand with his. He didn't mention the one hood still at large. He wasn't a threat, as he wasn't directly after Sara, but instead more of a threat to society as a whole. He'd leave that one to the police. "You're safe here. I wouldn't worry. We have decoys out to make him think you're leaving Morocco. With any luck we'll be able to catch him before he realizes that the decoys are just that."

"How do we end this?" Sara asked.

"There is no *we*," Talib said. "We have to put our son first. That means you staying here so I can protect him, and you."

He could see the anger flare in her gray eyes, and in the way she frowned at him.

"What do you think—"

"You've been doing the last two years…is that what you're going to say?" He squeezed her shoulder. "You've done a fine job of protecting him. Now it's my turn."

"But—"

"There's no choice, Sara," he interrupted. "If we want to keep Everett safe, no choice at all."

She looked at him and something softened in her look as they both realized that for the first time, he'd called his son by name.

Chapter Twenty-Seven

"Sara."

His tone was soft and yet strong and unhesitating. It carried a world of strength, the strength she'd run so far to come to. The strength she now feared. He could protect and destroy everything that she had. He was the devil and her savior, and he held her destiny in his strong, sun-bronzed hands. It was terrifying, it was…

It was as if he knew what she thought. And she wasn't sure how it happened, how she ended up in his arms. All she knew was that she didn't want to be there and couldn't move away.

As she looked into the passion sparkling in his eyes, she was drawn like she'd been so long ago. She ran a finger along his jawbone, wanting him, needing him as she always had. This time when he bent to kiss her, there was something different. Maybe it was the life they'd lived in the interim, or the boy they'd created. But the kiss was more intense, more passionate than anything she'd remembered before.

She tentatively reached up, her fingers threading through the curls that framed his face. It was an odd combination, that sun-bronzed, masculine face and the curls that seemed so soft in comparison.

Everett.

She pulled away at just the thought of her son. This was all too much, too inappropriate. It didn't matter that the boy was in another room or that he couldn't hear them or that he was asleep. None of it mattered.

She pushed him back and turned away from him, her arms folded beneath her breasts, her breath coming fast and her heart pounding.

"Sara," he said softly. "I'm sorry." His hand was on her shoulder as if that might make her turn around and face what she couldn't admit even to herself. It wasn't just about Everett anymore. She loved Talib and yet a relationship between them would never happen. She knew that. He'd thrown her to the curb once, she wouldn't allow it to happen again.

His hand was gentle but firm on her shoulder and she turned with the slight pressure. She saw the regret in his eyes and it was her undoing.

"That shouldn't have happened," he said softly. "I'm sorry."

Something inside her died at those words. Somehow, despite everything or maybe because of everything, she had hoped. That had been ridiculous. That hope had been a child's dream not that of a grown woman, especially that of a woman fighting to save her child. It was no longer about her. It hadn't been for a long time. Yet, for a moment back in Talib's arms, she had hoped.

"No worries," she said briskly as if the issue at hand was nothing more major than a broken dish.

She walked away from him and stopped at the window, where she could feel the solitude of the compound as it lay edged in darkness.

She'd only been here a short time, yet she hadn't gotten used to the silence.

"Sara," he said, interrupting her thoughts.

She turned slowly, reluctantly, as if facing him would reveal what she really felt, the feelings that she didn't even want to admit to herself.

"You're not making this easy," he said.

"What…" She wasn't sure where he was going with this. He'd been so clear three years ago. It was only now that she'd muddied the waters coming here, bringing Everett, that he seemed to have more on his mind.

"You do things to me. You always have."

She couldn't look at him. She didn't want him to dredge up feelings she'd never fully buried. "Don't say it."

"You don't know what I was going to say."

"Yes, I do. You don't want me. You want…"

"Sex?" He shook his head. "Is that what you think? It's not…"

She came over to him, drawn as she always was, as much as she tried to resist. She traced his cheek with her forefinger. "It's what I want." The words were soft and a surprise to both of them but especially her.

"Sara."

The blouse slipped off easily. He watched her. And

knowing that, even without looking up, meeting his eyes, he made her hot, made her want it more. The shoulder strap of her camisole slipped down as her thumb casually looped under it. She shut down the evil little voice in the back of her mind that told her to remember what had happened, despite protection, the last time. And with everything and all she'd been through, she wanted this—one last time.

"Sara." There was a thickness to his voice, a gravelly edge that wasn't normally there.

She moved closer.

"For old times' sake," she said and wondered where those words came from, whose voice that was. But heat ran through her and she only wanted him and she wanted him now.

He stood there as if she was no more interesting than any of the other pieces of furniture in this expansive room. She took another step and her breasts lightly touched his chest. The other strap dropped and the camisole slipped, revealing a lacy pink bra.

"Sara," he said again, as if her name was the only English word he knew, and he sounded slightly choked.

"Kiss me," she said softly as she reached up, taking his face in her hands, bringing him down to her as their lips met, soft, tentative. Everything inside her, the logic she refused to listen to, was screaming at her that this was insanity.

This time she didn't wait, she pulled him, unresisting, to her. She deepened the kiss, tasting him, feeling him hard against her before his arms tightened around her. This was what she wanted, what she knew they both wanted.

This was wrong, not the way it should be.

"No," she murmured, her hands moving to his shoulders, pushing him back.

He looked at her with troubled eyes.

She wanted him and yet she didn't. She wanted him for a short time and was terrified that her heart would make that a long time. She couldn't stand the heartache of losing him again. And she was fooling no one, herself least of all. She loved him and there was no going back.

She kissed him, hot and openmouthed, her body tight against his.

"I want you."

"You're sure?"

She didn't say anything, instead her hands slipped under his shirt and felt the silken skin and the sleek lines. His body was as hard and toned as she remembered. "I couldn't be more sure," she whispered.

It was hours later. She'd fallen asleep in his arms and now moonlight streamed across the bed and awakened her. She looked over to see him watching her.

"Sara." His voice was seductive in the waning hours of the night.

He leaned over and kissed her hard and deep. His hand was hot against her nipple. And passion eclipsed them again as his tongue worshiped her body and she begged him to enter her within minutes and end the sweet torture. They slept spooned together for what was left of the night and it was only the sunlight streaming across the room that awakened them.

Chapter Twenty-Eight

Talib left early that morning. She knew that he hoped to find a lead, to end this as soon as possible. In fact, he'd said as much. He'd been brisk and businesslike, but the kiss he had given her when he left had promised so much more.

Despite his absence, she knew that they were safe. Talib had made sure of that. When he wasn't there, there were trusted servants only a call away. There were three that she now knew well. Tazim, a middle-aged man with an easy smile, was the one she saw most frequently. In the last few days, he'd made a point of bringing a special treat for Everett every time he'd arrived. The fact that he checked on them three or four times a day and often dropped to his knees to briefly play with the boy had Everett chortling happily now at the sight of him.

After Talib had left, she'd been consumed with thoughts of what things might be like after this was over. Would she return to the States and take Everett with her, separate him from his father? Could she do that? She knew now that her fear could not shadow her son's life. He needed to know his father. She wasn't sure how she was going to make that happen. Could she endure months without her son while he was here and she was in the States? Not possible. He was too young to be wrenched from her in that way. But she couldn't fathom moving here, either.

She needed to get out, to get some air. Despite the vastness of this apartment—Talib had told her that it was four thousand square feet—she was restless. Her life was on hold. Her once busy days were now reduced to caring for Everett and worrying. It wasn't enough to keep either her mind or her soul occupied. It hadn't been for a long time. When she'd been on the run in the States, she couldn't use any of the management skills she trained for. Instead her drive and ambition had been reduced to a collection of menial jobs—salesclerk, a waitress at a bar and others she hardly remembered. Waitressing had been the best job as far as money. As long as she could handle the lewd comments and the fact that some drunk man was ogling her generous breasts, the tips were good. It wasn't the drunk trying to feel her up as she went by that ended that career. That one she handled with a well-placed elbow to the face. The one that ended it was the drunk who tried to accost her on her way to her car and scared her to death. The assault had been prevented by the intervention of an observant bouncer and had her turning in her waitress apron. It had been that job that had brought her to the brink and eventually here, when she realized that she couldn't run anymore.

She pushed away the thoughts of the events that had brought her here. She'd thought the whole process out one too many times in the planning and in the long hours in the hotel and now here. She had nothing to do but wait and it was driving her crazy. She'd ventured out of the suite of rooms that Talib had given her and Everett only a few times, and then only into the main quarters.

In some ways it seemed like they'd been here much longer. She was homesick but she had no home. She missed what was familiar. She missed the old life she'd once had in Casper, Wyoming, where she'd met and dated Talib.

That was all so long ago. In fact, months ago she'd given up the lease to her apartment. She'd done that when she'd first fled and put her things into storage. The items most important to her, she'd left with her parents. She'd contacted them regularly, which was how Tad had followed her. She'd stopped that once she'd learned from Talib how the app worked. Talib had given her access to a secure connection that had allowed her to let her family know that everything was fine. Interestingly, her mother had even been pleased at the fact that she was with Talib. But her mother had always liked him and she knew she'd secretly hoped, especially after the birth of Everett, that they'd get back together.

She thought of other things, of the tragedy of Tad. That just made her sad. That he'd turned bad, that he'd died, all of it. And thinking about it, she was angry, too. He'd had no right to do what he had done. But if none of it had happened she wouldn't have run to Talib. She wouldn't be here now knowing that she'd never stopped loving him. She wouldn't be here wondering if she had a chance.

She shivered as she looked out onto the lush grounds. It was a beautiful day, not too hot, not too cold. She looked back at the bookshelf. The books had spared her sanity. She'd thumbed through more books in the last hours than she could remember looking at in a long time. Maybe, at some point she'd have time to read them. Talib's sister had an eclectic taste that matched her own and she'd flipped through fiction and nonfiction with equal enthusiasm. Other than the books she'd felt awkward living in an apartment among someone else's things. And now, she felt like she was going stir-crazy.

It was early afternoon. Lunch was over and the day stretched out and with no clear objective to complete, it seemed endless. Everett had fallen asleep in the middle of the story she was reading him.

She settled down with a book but she couldn't concentrate. Her thoughts were everywhere. She wanted to be free to move around. She needed an objective, something to do. She was restless. One could only stay locked up for so long. She wasn't sure how zoo animals survived. But then she'd never believed in either the fairness or the rightness of locking another being up—even another species. That was why Everett had never been to a zoo in his young life, nor would he if she had any say.

Any say.

She put the book down, the words she'd just thought haunted her. It was the fear that one day, in her pursuit of her son's safety, she might give up her say in who he was and who he might become. One day, she might have no choice. It was her worst fear. It was why she'd kept him a secret when her heart knew she should have told Talib a long time ago. She didn't want to think about that. Instead, she forced herself to concentrate on other things, on the book she'd spent fifteen minutes selecting.

A little while later she nodded off.

"WE'VE GOT YOUR suspect who set the explosive device," Talib said as he leaned against the wall of Ian's office. "I just spoke to the police and they've made an arrest."

"That's a relief," Ian said, but he looked at Talib. "But it's not over, is it?"

"No. The suspect was hired by a man named Habib. No last name, at least not one that's available. I'm fairly certain it's the same man I've been investigating the last few days." He didn't go into details. Ian was a good friend, but there were some things he couldn't share. Something so critical to the investigation was one of them. In a way, keeping the information close to his chest protected everyone's best interest.

"I assume he's been arrested?" Ian asked.

"He has. I think Habib will be, too. It's only a matter of time. A very short time," he said.

"What about Sara?"

"She's safe," Talib replied.

"You're pretty closemouthed about this. But I get it. You're deep into a case." He stood up. "Look, they're upgrading some of the surveillance cameras this afternoon." He held out his hand. "Thanks for arranging that."

"We'll have you rock-solid by the end of next week," Talib said as he engaged in a brief handshake.

"Odd," Ian said. "Five days ago you were planning a joyride into the mountains. Now…"

"Everything has changed," Talib said.

"Everything," Ian replied. "But you'll make it right, man. You always do."

Chapter Twenty-Nine

"T," Emir said as soon as Talib answered his phone. "There's trouble at the compound."

"Damn, I'm nowhere near." Talib's jaw tightened. Emir was out of town. Because he was handling a code red case on his own Emir had compensated by continuing to field office calls. This call had come from their administrative and research backbone. If this hadn't been a code red, he would have taken on that duty in Emir's absence.

"The alarm just came in," Emir said. They had the security alarms feeding directly to the office. There, staff would immediately relay necessary information to Emir and any other relevant agents. It was a relay system that took mere seconds. Security was top priority. It was their livelihood and a service they sold. Their reputation hinged on the fact that it was as tight as it could be. But no security was airtight.

His grip on the phone tightened until he was threatening to break the plastic.

"The power's out, T. It went out exactly forty seconds ago. It appears there was a break in the line just outside the main fence, cutting off the entire compound. The generators should be cutting in immediately, but…"

"Even a few second delay is enough to breach the security," Talib said. This was unbelievable. They had considered every angle except this. "I'm five minutes away. Get the guardhouse on alert. Get them to secure…"

"I tried. There's no answer," Emir replied. "Drive like a sane man, T."

They were the last words Talib heard. He'd disconnected and was testing the limits of the BMW as he navigated the obstacle course of cars. He needed to get onto the freeway and make time. Five minutes away. It had to be less. He had to make it in four, three even. A truck pulled out in front of him.

He laid on the horn and the driver seemed to take that as a challenge and slowed slightly as a car passed him on either side, preventing him from pulling out. Finally, in what seemed like minutes but was only seconds, he was able to pull out and pass. He didn't bother giving the driver a look, a blast of the horn, anything. His concentration was solely on the road and on getting to the compound. And in all that time his mind could only think of Sara as he'd last seen her and Everett.

He had a son. He'd had little time with him and the fates couldn't be so cruel. Wouldn't be that cruel that he would lose him now. He'd get there on time or he'd die trying.

SARA WOKE WITH a start. She'd been napping like the very old or the very young, having fallen into a sleep that was deep and uninterrupted by dreams. The kind of sleep that had you waking up foggy, wondering where you were and how long you'd slept.

But something had awakened her. The book she'd been reading and that had slipped into her lap while she slept fell to the floor. She picked it up and set it on the small table beside the couch. She was still, listening, wondering what it was that had awakened her. There was no sound from down the hall, where Everett slept. But she knew it hadn't been him. It had been something else.

"Is anyone there?" she called, wondering if one of the servants had come to check on them or even if Talib had come back.

Silence.

Yet something wasn't right. She could feel the change in the air, like it was real and tangible when in fact there was nothing. She couldn't take any chances, especially considering all that had happened. Her instincts were on alert. Something was wrong. She couldn't see or hear it, but she could sense it.

She tiptoed to Everett's room and opened the door to peek in. The room he was in had no window. He was sound asleep. He was safe. Still, something wasn't right.

She went back to the main area. Again she heard something, a whisper of sound against the window. It was closed, but she knew something was off and she didn't like that she couldn't identify what it was.

It had to be one of the servants. She was just being paranoid, but despite how logical and safe that sounded, she was unable to convince herself. Her heart pounded as her imagination amplified the danger. She was backing up, putting herself between whatever her imagination was conjuring and her son.

"Hello?" She had to fight to keep the quaver out of her voice.

She knotted her fists and scanned the room, grabbing a tennis racket from a shelf at the bottom of the bookcase. It was out of place, something she'd meant to put back and another thing that had been rearranged by her busy son.

Everett.

She began to move more determinedly backward, toward his room, her eye remaining on the door. Should she call out? It was probably nothing. But the longer this went on, the more real it seemed to become.

Silence reigned. The seconds ticked by. She barely breathed but the sounds she heard just a few moments ago didn't repeat. It had been her imagination. She blew out a sigh of relief but still stood where she was, just in case.

Bushes rustled just outside the terrace doors.

She wanted to rush to Everett and yet something told her that would be the wrong thing to do. She was basing the thought purely on instinct. And other than the tennis racket, she was defenseless. But the logical side of her mind told her there were at least twenty-five people in this compound at any given time. The sheer numbers, never mind the security that was in place, made her feel safe.

It was nothing. She was being ridiculous. She looked over to where there was a call pad to page one of the servants or the guardhouse. It was usually lit up. She went to pick it up—nothing. It was dead. She grabbed her phone. She'd call the main number for the guardhouse. They might think she was crazy but she didn't care. Everett's safety was her main concern.

She had the phone in one hand and the racket under one arm when someone grabbed her around her neck and she was yanked back. The phone clattered to the tiles. Whoever it was, he was male, his arm thick and hairy. His hand was over her mouth and she was dragged through the apartment and down the hall that ran on the other side and away from Everett's room. She didn't scream, not wanting to awaken him, grateful that the danger was moving farther away from her son.

"Your boyfriend is a fool." The man's breath was like the rancid smell of rotted fish guts on her parents' dock. Something hard knocked against her temple. She could only assume that it was a gun.

She almost choked but instinct told her that would only enrage him. It took all her willpower not to.

"But then he always was, even when we were children."

He took his hand away from her mouth. "Who are you?" She struggled to regain some control, to stand up straight and take some of the pressure off the painful tugging of her hair that was caught beneath his arm, making her eyes water. Between that and his foul breath and the fear racing through her, she couldn't think. She needed to think, to get herself out of this jam and keep Everett safe.

The apartment was so large and initially, with Everett she liked to be close to him, and not being so had disconcerted her. Now she was glad for the distance. Everett couldn't hear what was going on, he wouldn't cry and bring attention to his presence.

But the moment she thought that, she heard him call her.

No, no, no, sweetheart. Ev, please no. Her head hurt as she tried to send the thoughts to her son. But she knew it was useless, she wasn't psychic and neither was her son.

"Your boy?" he asked almost pleasantly and went on without her answer. "Let's go get him," he said.

Instinct told her to play coy, to buy time. "Who?"

"Al-Nassar's heir."

"I have no idea who or what you're talking about."

"Your kid." He yanked her head back painfully by her hair and her eyes watered.

"He belongs to me."

"Tad said otherwise," he said. "I don't have time for this. Move." He pushed forward, not releasing his grip on her and making her stumble. "Give me the boy and I'll let you go."

Never, she thought. Play along, her sane, less panicked side told her. Buy time.

She heard scraping, what sounded like the murmur of voices—she wasn't sure. It was too faint. Maybe it was only her imagination. The door was old and heavy, the construction of the entire mansion such that sounds didn't travel well through closed doors.

Then she did what she told herself would only enrage him, but she needed to do something, because maybe in some way it would buy her some time.

She dug her nails into his hand and the grip around her neck only tightened and she choked.

In another hallway, yards away from her, Everett wailed.

She had to think. It was on her. She needed to get them out of this and she had no idea how.

Chapter Thirty

Talib's finger had been poised to ring the bell to the suite. This was Sara's home for now and he wouldn't invade it. Before he could press it, he heard his son crying. The baby monitor was hanging from his belt, where he'd put it yesterday and where it was whenever he was in the compound. He'd taken no chances with security, or so he'd thought until the power had gone out. Another minute and he knew it would be back up. It should have been back up already.

He frowned at the sound of his son's cries. Because the child wasn't crying at all. Instead they were shrieks of anger and frustration. Something was going on that he didn't like. He expected to hear Sara's voice comforting the boy. She never let him be upset for any length of time. She'd told him that she didn't think it was healthy.

Everett's cries escalated, but he heard nothing of Sara. Something wasn't right.

"Son of a…" Talib had his fingers on the keypad and unlocked the outer doors. But the key wouldn't go into the inside door's lock. It was jammed. Alarms were ringing in his head. All of this was pointing to something very wrong, something very bad. His family was in danger.

For a moment he was blinded by rage, but he soon had that under control and shifted into combat mode as he'd done so many times in his life. His family was inside and he was not stopping until they were safe and again under his watch.

Driving a shoulder into the door would do nothing. He knew that the door wouldn't budge. It was that well-built.

He pulled the Glock from his hip and stood back. He used his forearm to cover his eyes and as much of his face as possible as he stood slightly sideways and fired once, twice. He blew a hole through the lock and flipped the knob, bursting into the room.

He could hear voices in the corridor to his left, away from the boy. Relief and rage collided. The boy's room was in the opposite direction. He might be safe. Was Sara?

He had his gun in both hands and he led with the weapon as he turned into the corridor.

The man Talib faced was not the boy he remembered. He'd obviously lived a hard life in the interim, hard and bitter from the looks of the deep lines and the hateful twist of his mouth. But it was who he had by the neck that terrified Talib.

"I didn't expect you," Habib said, the gun he held to Sara's head not wavering for an instant.

"I'm sure you didn't," Talib said calmly as he lowered the gun.

"Give me the money and she lives," Habib snarled as his eyes met Talib's. "You gave a quarter of what I asked. What do you think I am, a fool?"

"Certainly not," Talib said carefully.

"Certainly not," he replied, mocking Talib's careful diction. "Quit making bloody fun of me. You and your rich-kid attitude."

It was like he was slipping back into childhood and using terms he might have used as a boy.

"I would never make fun of you," Talib said. "I'll get the money…" He met Sara's eyes. He wanted to give her a signal, tell her that it was all right. That he'd make it all right no matter what it took. She and Everett would be fine. But he couldn't say any of that, he could only try to communicate some of it with a look.

She blinked, slowly, carefully, as if telling him that she understood.

"Certainly, I can give you money. How much? I'm always happy to help someone in need. Even though I have no tie to the kid."

"Certainly, nothing," Habib said in a raised voice that had a snarl edging through it. "I'm taking the boy, there's nothing you can do to stop me. You can have him back when I get the money."

He met Sara's eyes. There was something sparking in them that reflected more determination than panic. Habib had her by the throat and he could see the red handprint on her cheek where he'd hit her. Down the opposite hall, Everett continued to scream for his mother.

It was a horrific scene. His family was on the edge

of destruction because of a madman. He needed to think his way out of this. But options had been eliminated. There were no guns blazing, no hand-to-hand battle. The mother of his son stood between those two options.

"Take him. Take the kid if you want," Talib said and Sara looked at him with horror. "I was willing to help once. But twice." He shrugged. "It's not like my heart's in it."

He tried not to meet her eyes after that. He could only hope that she'd realize what he was trying to do.

"What are you saying?" Habib scowled.

"I don't want him. He was born out of wedlock. Did you know that?" He put his gun back in its holster and ran a hand through his hair as he attempted to look put out and casual. "There's no guarantee he's even mine. In fact, I have serious doubts…"

"Shut up!" Habib screamed. "Just shut up. He's yours."

"I'm not on the birth certificate," Talib said calmly, but his heart beat at an insane rate. He couldn't look at Sara, could only hope that her silence was confirmation that she realized what he was doing and was playing along. "Besides that, any kid of mine wouldn't be that ugly."

"You're playing me."

"You're the lucky one, Habib. You got out of the establishment. Away from the users like her."

Silence was heavy between them. He kept eye contact with Habib. It was one of the hardest things he'd ever done.

"Don't make me repeat it. If you want the kid, take him. As you can hear, all he does is scream. I want nothing to do with him. Take her, too." The words stuck on his lips. They were the most difficult words he'd ever said. But they were having an effect, he could see the doubt on his opponent's face.

"You want me to take the kid?" Habib scowled as if what Talib had been saying was finally registering. He wasn't holding Sara as tightly against him as his face reflected his doubts.

Talib shrugged. Finally, he looked at Sara, saw the tears that shimmered, but her lips turned slightly up. It was a signal that she was with him. "Why don't you show us that birth certificate and prove once and for all that you're just another conniving gold digger?" Talib said to Sara as he glared at her and mentally begged her to stay strong.

She didn't drop her gaze, only the slight smile was gone. "I needed the money," she said softly.

"Sure you did," he snarled. "I'm sick of her. Take her if you want."

He looked at Habib. "You know I envied you. You never had these problems with women like her. I don't know if any woman ever liked me for me. Seriously, this one's a doozy, the kid really is uglier than sin."

He looked at Sara. "Get the birth certificate, show him," he demanded in a voice that was lethal. "If nothing else, get the brat's passport."

Sara's eyes met his and something—an understanding—passed between them, almost as electric as the passion they'd so recently rediscovered. It was brief, and as quickly as they disconnected, she sank her teeth into her captor's forearm and, at the same time, pushed away from his grip. It wasn't much. There was a split second of time that was all it would take for Habib to regain control.

It was all Talib needed. He pulled his gun. He aimed even as he said that one important word to the woman he knew he loved. "Run."

He didn't have to say more. There was only one place for her to run. Straight to their son, where she would protect him with her life.

He only had an instant, but it was enough. One shot took out Habib.

He couldn't let his thoughts stray any further than that. Habib was down and he wasn't moving. Blood pooled around his head. He strode over, pushed him with his foot, then leaned down and put the back of his hand under his nostrils. Nothing. He checked his pulse for good measure.

"Dead," he said with satisfaction and pulled an afghan off the back of the couch and dropped it over the body. It wasn't a matter of respect but rather an act of protection. He didn't want his son's innocence destroyed by the sight, or the woman he loved traumatized any more than she already had been.

This kind of thing was his world. For a short time, it had been theirs. It was up to him to make sure it never happened again.

Chapter Thirty-One

"It's finally over, sweetheart," Talib said to Sara. It was a few hours later. The police had completed their questioning and the body had been removed. In the midst of all that, Everett had been placed under the watchful care of Andre. When she'd last checked, Andre had parked the boy with him in the kitchen, where the staff were being entertained by the toddler's antics. There were more volunteer guards and nannies in that kitchen than a state prison. Even if there was a threat, Talib had no doubt that it would be handled.

"What do we do now?" Sara asked.

It wasn't about the two of them. They both knew that she asked because of their son. He was the one unspoken agreement between them. They'd both do whatever it took to protect him and that meant giving him what was best for him in all things.

"You'll want to see him."

"Of course," Talib said easily. "But I want to see his mother, too."

"What do you mean?"

"I love you, Sara. I think I always have. I…" He paused and rephrased his words. "We should never have broken up."

"It was your doing." She shook her head as if remembering the experience. "Although, I think I might have had my moments."

"No, you're right. It was my fault. If I'd hung in there, we would have been a family. I wouldn't have missed…"

"I'm so sorry, Talib. If I could do it over—"

"I know," he said, cutting her off. He put a hand on her shoulder. "There's so much more I know about you, sweetheart, and oddly about myself that I've learned since you came back into my life."

"Can you forgive me?"

"Not that long ago I would have never forgiven you," Talib said darkly. "What you did was incomprehensible. At least that's how I would have seen it even a year ago and how I saw it when you first told me. I see it a little differently now. I guess, I see your side, or at least some of it."

"I wouldn't forgive me," she said softly.

"You're not me," Talib replied. "I'm willing to forgive if you are."

She stood up, her hands twisted behind her back. She couldn't look at him. She didn't want to admit the real reason that she'd kept them apart. Her fear had been that great. They couldn't reach an agreement if she wasn't honest with herself, with Talib.

Fear. That's all it had been, but it wasn't such a small thing for it had stolen two years of a father's time with his son. It was unforgiveable and in an odd way she thought she might feel worse about it than Talib.

"I was afraid."

"Were you that afraid of me?" Talib asked darkly. "What did I do?" He stood up, his hands opening wide as he made an expansive gesture that seemed to include her and the empty room at large.

"You didn't do anything," she said softly, although she thought of the breakup and realized that that wasn't completely true. She'd harbored some resentment toward him over that. But that wasn't the reason for everything that came down after that point. "It was about who you are. Who your family is."

"My family?" His dark brows drew together and, for a minute, there was silence between them. "You mean our wealth." It wasn't a question. They both knew that was part of the problem. He hadn't needed to ask.

"Part of it," she said softly. "Your influence. All of it."

"Everett is part of that."

"I know. And I planned for you to know of him someday. I just didn't want..."

"This is about custody, isn't it?" He scowled. "I don't believe this. You thought..."

"It wasn't like that. It—"

"You came here believing that you would lose him," Talib said in a soft voice that was underscored with a steely determination. Somehow he had closed the gap between them and now he stood just to her left, behind her, too large, too imposing, too close.

His hand touched her shoulder, heavy and solid, as he turned her around to face him, closing the last bit of safety, of distance, between them.

"It was a reprehensible thing you did," he said softly.

Her heart broke at the words.

"But it took real courage to come here." He cupped her face between his hands. "Your sense of right won over."

"It was what Ev needed," she said quietly. She looked up, met his eyes. Usually so guarded, they now seemed to reflect a piece of his soul. "It was what you both needed."

"It was what *we* needed," he said in a thick whisper. "Everett needs to know who he is and where he comes from. He needs to spend time in Morocco."

"With you?"

"Exactly. But not by himself, of course," he quickly assured her. "He's too young to be without his mother."

"What are you suggesting?"

He took both her hands in his. "I want to try again, Sara, with us. I want us to be good parents to our son. Together—here, in Morocco."

"My career?" She blushed. They both knew her management career had dead-ended in the States along with her dream to own a bed-and-breakfast, as she'd fled from state to state.

"Ian is in desperate need of a manager. Someone who knows the business. I mentioned…"

"You didn't?" She felt a sudden sense of relief.

"I did."

"I don't have a work visa," she said, realizing the silliness of such a comment. She was speaking to an Al-Nassar. She didn't doubt that paperwork would not be an issue. They lived in a different world than other beings, it had been part of what had torn them apart.

"I love you," he said simply.

"I've never stopped loving you," she said.

"You've never said that before."

"I was afraid you'd never say it back," she replied. For it was true—what did she have to offer an Al-Nassar? She had nothing that he wanted but his son.

"I'd marry you whether you had Everett or not," he said. "In fact, I'd have married you three years ago if one of us hadn't botched things up."

"Talib." She punched him lightly in the chest.

He leaned down and kissed her, hot and hard and passionately, and it told her everything she needed to know and everything he felt. She melted into him and into the promise of that kiss, knowing that the future would be much different than she'd imagined. It would be a future, that, once, so unbelievably long ago, she'd dreaded.

Epilogue

Three months later

The move had been less difficult than Sara had imagined. She'd never considered traveling anywhere. Not in her previous life and definitely nowhere as exotic as Morocco. She'd never thought of living anywhere other than Wyoming. Since becoming a mother, the focus of her thoughts had been what was best for her son. He needed his father. The events of the last months had proven that. More importantly, both her son and his father had roots here. It was a pull that was undeniable. It was a land that belonged to both of them and, as a result, belonged to her, as well.

But Talib had rocked everything when he'd announced only a few days ago that he wanted to join his brother Faisal in the Wyoming branch of Nassar Security.

After everything that had transpired, she'd been ready to stay in Morocco for a while, even for the duration of Everett's childhood, if that's what it took to make their family feel whole. But Talib had insisted that while his son needed to know his family, he was fine with raising him in Wyoming with visits to Morocco. Sara was overjoyed—Wyoming was where she grew up and, truthfully, the thought of returning was something she'd never anticipated and filled her with joy. Morocco had been an experience, a place she was willing to stay for the good of her son, but Wyoming was what she knew and, before she met Talib, what made her feel safe. Going home was the ultimate gift.

The time they'd spent in the compound had, in an odd way, been like a trial marriage. But it was the patient wooing that Talib had done, the thoughtful dates that always factored in what her interests and passions were, dates he'd arranged over the weeks when the horror in their lives had finally ended. When life calmed down he'd also spent time alone with their son. Taking him out on what he called boy trips, which Everett loved. Sara also enjoyed the time alone. He was thoughtful in every way, a natural father. But it was as a lover that he totally won her over. Not, if she really wanted to admit it, that he needed to win her over. She'd always loved him and even after everything that had happened, she'd always trusted him. He'd been who she'd turn to in what had looked like her darkest hour.

It had been a surprise to learn he had felt the same.

But it was the ring on her finger that early winter evening over a private supper that had convinced her more than Talib's words. Even though his words meant everything.

As his lips met hers, she knew that it meant everything to Talib, too.

"It's not official," he whispered against her lips. "But the three of us are a family.

"Sara Al-Nassar," he whispered.

"Elliott," she whispered back. "I'll save Al-Nassar for you and the baby."

"As long as you're mine," he said.

"Deal," she whispered back and his tongue opened her lips with a gentle caress and they both knew that the name meant nothing and everything.

"Unless you wanted to argue now and make up with a little loving…"

"Talib," she giggled and curled up against him. "Al-Nassar and Elliott, that's a lot of family."

"A whole lot of family," he agreed.

* * * * *

Check out the previous books in the
DESERT JUSTICE series:

SHEIK'S RULE
SHEIK'S RESCUE

And don't miss the thrilling conclusion in

SHEIK DEFENSE

Available soon from Harlequin Intrigue!

DARBY CAHILL ADJUSTED his Stetson as he moved toward the bandstand. The streets of Gilt Edge, Montana, were filled with revelers who'd come to celebrate the yearly chokecherry harvest on this beautiful day. The main street had been blocked off for all the events. People had come from miles around for the celebration of a cherry that was so tart it made your mouth pucker.

As he climbed the steps, Darby figured it just proved that people would celebrate anything. Normally, his twin sister, Lillie, attended, but this year she was determined that he should do more of their promotion at these events.

"I hate it as much as you do," she'd assured him. "But believe me, you'll get more attention up there on the stage than me. Just say a few words, throw T-shirts into the crowd, have some fry bread and come home. You can do this." Clearly, she knew his weakness for fry bread as well as his dislike of being the center of attention.

The T-shirts were from the Stagecoach Saloon, the bar and café the two of them owned and operated outside town. Since it had opened, the bar had helped sponsor the Chokecherry Festival each year.

He heard his name being announced and sighed as he made his way up the rest of the steps to the microphone to deafening applause. He tipped his hat to the crowd, swallowed the lump in his throat and said, "It's an honor to be here and to be part of such a wonderful celebration."

"Are you taking part in the pit-spitting competition?" someone yelled from the crowd, and others joined in. Along with being bitter, chokecherries were mostly pit.

"I'm going to leave that to the professionals," he said, reaching for the box of T-shirts, wanting this over with as quickly as possible. He didn't like being in the spotlight any longer than he had to. Also, he hoped that once he started throwing the shirts, everyone would forget about the pit-spitting contest later.

He was midthrow when he spotted a woman in the crowd. What had caught his eye was the brightly colored scarf around her dark hair. It fluttered in the breeze, giving him glimpses of only her face.

He let go and the T-shirt sailed through the air as if caught on the breeze. He saw with a curse that it was headed right for the woman. Grimacing, he watched the rolled up T-shirt clip the woman's shoulder.

She looked up, clearly startled. He had the impression of serious, dark eyes, full lips. Their gazes locked for an instant and he felt something like lightning pierce his heart. For a moment, he couldn't breathe. Rooted to the spot, all he could hear was the drumming of his heart, the roaring crowd a dull hum in the background.

Someone behind the woman in the crowd scooped up the T-shirt and, scarf fluttering, the woman turned away, disappearing into the throng of people.

What had *that* been about? His heart was still pounding. What had he seen in those bottomless dark eyes that left him…breathless? He knew what Lillie would have said. Love at first sight. Something he would have scoffed at—just moments ago.

"Do you want me to help you?" a voice asked at his side.

Darby nodded to the festival volunteer. He threw another T-shirt, looking in the crowd for the woman. She was gone.

Once the box of T-shirts was empty, he hurriedly stepped off the stage into the moving mass. His job was done. His plan was to have some fry bread and then head back to the saloon. He was happiest behind the bar. Or on the back of a horse. Being Montana born and raised in open country, crowds made him nervous.

The main street had been blocked off and now booths lined both sides of the street all the way up the hill that led out of town. Everywhere he looked there were chokecherry T-shirts and hats, dish towels and coffee mugs. Most chokecherries found their way into wine or syrup or jelly, but today he could have purchased the berries in lemonade or pastries or even barbecue sauce. He passed stands of fresh fruit and vegetables, crafts of all kinds and every kind of food.

As he moved through the swarm of bodies now filling the downtown street, the scent of fry bread in the air, he couldn't help searching for the woman. That had been the strangest experience he'd ever had. He told himself it could have been heatstroke had the day been hotter. Also, he felt perfectly fine now.

He didn't want to make more of it than it was, and yet, he'd give anything to see her again. As crazy as it sounded, he couldn't throw off the memory of that sharp hard shot to his heart when their gazes had met.

As he worked his way through the crowd, following the smell of fry bread, he watched for the colorful scarf the woman had been wearing. He needed to know what that was about earlier. He told himself he was being ridiculous, but if he got a chance to see her again…

Someone in the crowd stumbled against his back. He caught what smelled like lemons in the air as a figure started to brush by him. Out of the corner of his eye, he saw the colorful scarf wrapped around her head of dark hair.

Like a man sleepwalking, he grabbed for the end of the scarf as it fluttered in the breeze. His fingers closed on the silken fabric, but only for a second. She was moving fast enough that his fingers lost purchase and dropped to her arm.

In midstep, she half turned toward him, his sudden touch slowing her. In those few seconds, he saw her face, saw her startled expression. He had the bizarre thought that this woman was in trouble. Without realizing it, he tightened his grip on her arm.

Her eyes widened in alarm. It all happened in a manner of seconds. As she tried to pull away, his hand slid down the silky smooth skin of her forearm until it caught on the wide bracelet she was wearing on her right wrist.

Something dropped from her hand as she jerked free of his hold. He heard a snap and her bracelet came off in his hand. His gaze went to the thump of whatever she'd dropped as it hit the ground. Looking down, he saw what she'd dropped. *His wallet?*

Astonishment rocketed through him as he realized that when she'd bumped into him from behind, she'd picked his pocket! Feeling like a fool, he bent to retrieve his wallet. Jostled by the meandering throng, he quickly rose and tried to find her, although he wasn't sure what exactly he planned to do when he did. Music blared from a Western band over the roar of voices.

He stood holding the woman's bracelet in one hand and his wallet in the other, looking for the bright scarf in the mass of gyrating festivalgoers.

She was gone.

Darby stared down at his wallet, then at the strange, large, gold-tinted cuff bracelet and laughed at his own foolishness. His moment of "love at first sight" had been with a *thief*? A two-bit pickpocket? Wouldn't his family love this!

Just his luck, he thought as he pocketed his wallet and considered what to do with what appeared to be heavy, cheap, costume jewelry. He'd been lucky. He'd gotten off easy in more ways than one. His first thought was to chuck the bracelet into the nearest trash can and put the whole episode behind him.

But he couldn't quite shake the feeling he'd gotten when he'd looked into her eyes—or when he'd realized the woman was a thief. Telling himself it wouldn't hurt to keep a reminder of his close call, he slipped the bracelet into his jacket pocket.

MARIAH AYERS GRABBED her bare wrist, the heat of the man's touch still tingling there. What wasn't there was her prized bracelet, she realized with a start. Her heart dropped. She hadn't taken the bracelet off since her grandmother had put it on her, making her promise never to part with it.

This will keep you safe and bring you luck, Grandmother Loveridge had promised on her deathbed. *Be true to who you are.*

She fought the urge to turn around in the surging throng of people, go find him and demand he give it back. But she knew she couldn't do that for fear of being arrested. Or worse. So much for the bracelet bringing her luck, she thought, heart heavy. She had no choice but to continue moving as she was swept up in the flowing crowd. Maybe she could find a high spot where she could spot her mark. And then what?

Mariah figured she'd cross that bridge when she came to it. Pulling off her scarf, she shoved it into her pocket. It was a great device for misdirection— normally—but now it would be a dead giveaway.

Ahead, she spotted stairs and quickly climbed half a dozen steps at the front of a bank to stop and look back.

The street was a sea of cowboy hats. One cowboy looked like another to her. How would she ever be able to find him—let alone get her bracelet back given that by now he would know what she'd been up to? She hadn't even gotten a good look at him. Shaken and disheartened, she told herself she would do whatever it took. She desperately needed that bracelet back—and not just for luck or sentimental reasons. It was her ace in the hole.

Two teenagers passed, arguing over which one of them got the free T-shirt they'd scored. She thought of the cowboy she'd seen earlier up on the stage, the one throwing the T-shirts. He'd looked right at her. Their gazes had met and she'd felt as if he had seen into her dark heart—if not her soul.

No wonder she'd blown a simple pick. She was rusty at this, clearly, but there had been a time when she could recall each of her marks with clarity. She closed her eyes. Nothing. Squeezing them tighter, she concentrated.

With a start, she recalled that his cowboy hat had been a light gray. She focused on her mark's other physical attributes. Long legs clad in denim, slim hips, muscular thighs, broad shoulders. A very nice behind. She shook off that image. A jean jacket over a pale blue checked shirt. Her pickpocketing might not be up to par, but at least there was nothing wrong with her memory, she thought as she opened her eyes and again scanned the crowd. Her uncle had taught her well.

But she needed more. She closed her eyes again.

She'd gotten only a glimpse of his face when he'd grabbed first her scarf and then her arm. Her eyes flew open as she had a thought. He must have been on to to her immediately. Had she botched the pick that badly? She really *was* out of practice.

She closed her eyes again and tried to concentrate over the sound of the two teens still arguing over the T-shirt. Yes, she'd seen his face. A handsome, rugged face and pale eyes. Not blue. No. Gray? Yes. With a start she realized where she'd seen him before. It was the man from the bandstand, the one who'd thrown the T-shirt and hit her. She was sure of it.

"Excuse me, I'll buy that T-shirt from you," she said, catching up to the two teens as they took their squabble off toward a burger stand.

They both turned to look at her in surprise. "It's not for sale," said one.

The other asked, "How much?"

"Ten bucks."

"No way."

"You got it for *free*," Mariah pointed out, only to have both girls' faces freeze in stubborn determination.

"Fine, twenty."

"Make it thirty," the greedier of the two said.

She shook her head as she dug out the money. Her grandmother would have given them the evil eye. Or threatened to put some kind of curse on them. "You're thieves, you know that?" she said as she grabbed the T-shirt before they could take off with it *and* her money.

Escaping down one of the side streets, she finally got a good look at what was printed across the front of the T-shirt. Stagecoach Saloon, Gilt Edge, Montana.

LILLIE CAHILL HESITATED at the back door of the Stagecoach Saloon. It had been a stagecoach stop back in the 1800s when gold had been coming out of the mine at Gilt Edge. Each stone in the saloon's walls, like each of the old wooden floorboards inside, had a story. She'd often wished the building could talk.

When the old stagecoach stop had come on the market, she had jumped at purchasing it, determined to save the historical two-story stone building. It had been her twin's idea to open a bar and café. She'd been skeptical at first, but trusted Darby's instincts. The place had taken off.

Lately, she felt sad just looking at the place.

Until recently, she'd lived upstairs in the remodeled apartment. She'd moved in when they bought the old building and had made it hers by collecting a mix of furnishings from garage sales and junk shops. This had not just been her home. It was her heart, she thought, eyes misting as she remembered the day she'd moved out.

Since her engagement to Trask Beaumont and the completion of their home on the ranch, she'd given up her apartment to her twin, Darby. He had been living in a cabin not far from the bar, but he'd jumped at the chance to live upstairs.

Now she glanced toward the back window. The curtains were some she'd left when she'd moved out.

One of them flapped in the wind. Darby must have left the window open. She hadn't been up there to see what he'd done with the place. She wasn't sure she wanted to know, since she'd moved most everything out, leaving it pretty much a blank slate. She thought it might still be a blank slate, knowing her brother.

Pushing open the back door into the bar kitchen, she was met with the most wonderful of familiar scents. Fortunately, not everything had changed in her life, she thought, her mood picking up some as she entered the warm café kitchen.

"Tell me those are your famous enchiladas," she said to Billie Dee, their heavyset, fiftysomething Texas cook.

"You know it, sugar," the cook said with a laugh. "You want me to dish you up a plate? I've got home-made pinto beans and some Spanish rice like you've never tasted."

"You mean *hotter* than I've ever tasted."

"Oh, you Montanans. I'll toughen you up yet."

Lillie laughed. "I'd love a plate." She pulled out a chair at the table where the help usually ate in the kitchen and watched Billie Dee fill two plates.

"So how are the wedding plans coming along?" the cook asked as she joined her at the table.

"I thought a simple wedding here with family and friends would be a cinch," Lillie said as she took a bite of the enchilada. She closed her eyes for a moment, savoring the sweet and then hot bite of peppers before all the other flavors hit her. She groaned softly. "These are the best you've ever made."

"Bless your heart," Billie Dee said, smiling. "I take it the wedding has gotten more complicated?"

"I can't get married without my father and who knows when he'll be coming out of the mountains." Their father, Ely Cahill, was a true mountain man now who spent most of the year up in the mountains either panning for gold or living off the land. He'd given up ranching after their mother had died and had turned the business over to her brothers Hawk and Cyrus.

Their oldest brother, Tucker, had taken off at eighteen. They hadn't seen or heard from him since. Their father was the only one who wasn't worried about him.

Tuck needs space. He's gone off to find himself. He'll come home when he's ready, Ely had said.

The rest of the family hadn't been so convinced. But if Tuck was anything like their father, they would have heard something from the cops. Ely had a bad habit of coming out of the mountains thirsty for whiskey—and ending up in their brother Sheriff Flint Cahill's jail. Who knew where Tuck was. Lillie didn't worry about him. She had four other brothers to deal with right here in Gilt Edge.

"I can see somethin's botherin' you," Billie Dee said now.

Lillie nodded. "Trask insists we wait to get married since he hopes to have the finishing touches on the house so we can have the reception there."

Trask, the only man she'd ever loved, had come back into her life after so many years that she'd thought she'd never see him again. But they'd found their way back together and now he was building a house for them on the ranch he'd bought not far from the bar.

"Waitin' sounds reasonable," the cook said between bites.

"I wish we'd eloped."

"Something tells me the wedding isn't the problem," Billie Dee said, using her fork to punctuate her words.

"I'll admit it's been hard giving up my apartment upstairs. I put so much love into it."

"Darby will take good care of it."

Don't miss
OUTLAW'S HONOR,
available June 2017 wherever
HQN Books and ebooks are sold.

www.Harlequin.com

INTRIGUE

Available June 20, 2017

#1719 HUNTED
Killer Instinct • by Cynthia Eden
Cassandra "Casey" Quinn has been eluding the clutches of a brutal killer. John Duvane, former navy SEAL and current member of the FBI's elite Underwater Search and Evidence Response Team, may just be fearless enough to save her.

#1720 MARRIAGE CONFIDENTIAL
by Debra Webb & Regan Black
Madison Goode's PR career is at an all-time high—until everything she's worked for comes under threat. She turns to old friend Sam Bellemere, cocreator of the world's most secure cyber system, but will he be willing to help when he discovers she's listed him as her husband?

#1721 HOT RESOLVE
Ballistic Cowboys • by Elle James
Hot-tempered US Marine Rex "T-Rex" Trainor didn't plan on falling for pretty caregiver Sierra Daniels, not while an explosive situation demands everything he has to give to Homeland Security.

#1722 UNDERCOVER HUSBAND
The Ranger Brigade: Family Secrets • by Cindi Myers
Scientist Hannah Dietrich is a logical thinker used to looking after herself, but when her sister dies after joining self-proclaimed prophet Daniel Metwater's "Family" and her infant niece goes missing, she'll go undercover with sexy agent Walt Riley, a member of the Ranger Brigade who just may open her heart as they crack the case.

#1723 POLICE PROTECTOR
The Lawmen: Bullets and Brawn • by Elizabeth Heiter
Ever since a shooting drove Shaye Mallory to quit her job as a computer forensics technician, detective Cole Walker has been determined to get her back in the department. But when another shooter appears, Cole will have to protect her around the clock to keep her safe from the unknown threat.

#1724 SHEIK DEFENSE
Desert Justice • by Ryshia Kennie
Sheik Faisal Al-Nassar never forgot Ava Adams, but he didn't expect the next time he saw her, he'd be pulling her out of a life raft in the middle of the Atlantic Ocean. With her life on the line and her memory gone, can Ava trust Faisal to rescue her over and over again?

SPECIAL EXCERPT FROM

⊕ HARLEQUIN®

INTRIGUE

*Madison Goode knows just the man for the job to stop
a cybersecurity breach at an art museum reception—
but why is he on the guest list as her husband?*

*Read on for a sneak preview of
MARRIAGE CONFIDENTIAL,
by* USA TODAY *bestselling authors*
Debra Webb *and* **Regan Black***!*

She glanced up and down the hallway before meeting
his gaze. "Spend a few minutes at the reception with
me. News of my, um, husband's arrival has made people
curious."

He kept her waiting, but she didn't flinch. "Okay, on
one condition."

"Only one?"

He reconsidered his position. "One condition and I
reserve the right to add conditions based on your answers."

She held her ground and his gaze. "I reserve the right to
refuse on a per item basis. Name your primary condition."

He felt the smile curl his lips, saw her lovely mouth
curve in reply. "Tell me where and why we married."

"Not here." Her smile faded. "You deserve a full
explanation and you'll get it, I promise. As soon as I
navigate the minefield this evening has become. I don't
have any right to impose further, but I could use a buffer
in there."

He suddenly wanted to step up and be that buffer. For her. "I'm no asset in social settings, Madison."

"No one's expecting you to be a social butterfly. You only have to be yourself and pretend to be proud of me."

He didn't care for her phrasing. Before he could debate the terms further, she leaned her body close to his and gave him a winning smile. "Later," she murmured, tapping his lips with her finger. "Let's go. There's only an hour left." She linked her hand with his and turned, giving a start when they came face-to-face with one of the guests.

Her moves made sense now. She'd known they were being watched while he'd been mesmerized by her soft green eyes. The intimacy had only been for show. Thank goodness.

The only thing that came naturally to him was demonstrating pride in his fake wife. She had a flare for diplomacy—no surprise, considering her career. He admired her ability to say the right things or politely evade questions she didn't want to answer.

When they entered the gallery where the prized white jade cup glowed under soft lights surrounded by guards, he was the only person close enough to catch her relieved sigh. She squeezed his hand. "Thank you, Sam. You saved me tonight."

Don't miss
MARRIAGE CONFIDENTIAL,
available July 2017 wherever
Harlequin® Intrigue books and ebooks are sold.

www.Harlequin.com

HIEXP0617

EXCLUSIVE LIMITED TIME OFFER AT
www.HARLEQUIN.com

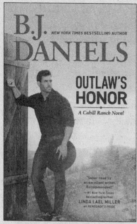

$7.99 U.S./$9.99 CAN.

$1.⁰⁰ OFF

New York Times Bestselling Author

B.J. DANIELS
OUTLAW'S HONOR

She never expected this Cahill to be
her hero—or the only man she'd need.

*Available May 30, 2017.
Get your copy today!*

Receive **$1.00 OFF** the purchase price of
OUTLAW'S HONOR by B.J. Daniels
when you use the coupon code below on Harlequin.com.

OUTLAW1

Offer valid from May 30, 2017, until June 30, 2017, on www.Harlequin.com.
Valid in the U.S.A. and Canada only. To redeem this offer, please add the print or
ebook version of OUTLAW'S HONOR by B.J. Daniels to your shopping cart and
then enter the coupon code at checkout.

DISCLAIMER: Offer valid on the print or ebook version of OUTLAW'S HONOR by
B.J. Daniels from May 30, 2017, at 12:01 a.m. ET until June 30, 2017, 11:59 p.m.
ET at www.Harlequin.com only. The Customer will receive $1.00 OFF the list price
of OUTLAW'S HONOR by B.J. Daniels in print or ebook on www.Harlequin.com
with the **OUTLAW1** coupon code. Sales tax applied where applicable. Quantities
are limited. Valid in the U.S.A. and Canada only. All orders subject to approval.

HQN
www.HQNBooks.com

® and ™ are trademarks owned and used by the trademark owner and/or its licensee.
© 2017 Harlequin Enterprises Limited

PHCOUPBJDHI0617

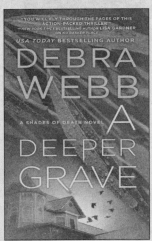

THE WORLD IS BETTER WITH

Romance

Harlequin has everything from contemporary, passionate and heartwarming to suspenseful and inspirational stories.

Whatever your mood, we have a romance just for you!

Get 2 Free Books,
Plus 2 Free Gifts—
just for trying the Reader Service!

YES! Please send me 2 FREE Harlequin® Intrigue novels and my 2 FREE gifts (gifts are worth about $10 retail). After receiving them, if I don't wish to receive any more books, I can return the shipping statement marked "cancel." If I don't cancel, I will receive 6 brand-new novels every month and be billed just $4.99 each for the regular-print edition or $5.74 each for the larger-print edition in the U.S., or $5.74 each for the regular-print edition or $6.49 each for the larger-print edition in Canada. That's a savings of at least 12% off the cover price! It's quite a bargain! Shipping and handling is just 50¢ per book in the U.S. and 75¢ per book in Canada.* I understand that accepting the 2 free books and gifts places me under no obligation to buy anything. I can always return a shipment and cancel at any time. Even if I never buy another book, the two free books and gifts are mine to keep forever.

Please check one: ☐ Harlequin® Intrigue Regular-Print   ☐ Harlequin® Intrigue Larger-Print
(182/382 HDN GLP2)   (199/399 HDN GLP3)

Name _____ (PLEASE PRINT)

Address _____ Apt. #

City _____ State/Prov. _____ Zip/Postal Code _____

Signature (if under 18, a parent or guardian must sign)

Mail to the **Reader Service**:
IN U.S.A.: P.O. Box 1867, Buffalo, NY 14240-1867
IN CANADA: P.O. Box 611, Fort Erie, Ontario L2A 9Z9

*Terms and prices subject to change without notice. Prices do not include applicable taxes. Sales tax applicable in N.Y. Canadian residents will be charged applicable taxes. Offer not valid in Quebec. This offer is limited to one order per household. Books received may not be as shown. Not valid for current subscribers to Harlequin Intrigue books. All orders subject to credit approval. Credit or debit balances in a customer's account(s) may be offset by any other outstanding balance owed by or to the customer. Please allow 4 to 6 weeks for delivery. Offer available while quantities last.

Your Privacy—The Reader Service is committed to protecting your privacy. Our Privacy Policy is available online at www.ReaderService.com or upon request from the Reader Service.

We make a portion of our mailing list available to reputable third parties that offer products we believe may interest you. If you prefer that we not exchange your name with third parties, or if you wish to clarify or modify your communication preferences, please visit us at www.ReaderService.com/consumerchoice or write to us at Reader Service Preference Service, P.O. Box 9062, Buffalo, NY 14240-9062. Include your complete name and address.

HI17